. . . then came wandering by
A shadow like an angel, with bright hair
Dabbled in blood. . . .

King Richard III

Upstairs at last, and in her bed and the house darkened and all quiet, Mrs. Moffat let herself entertain a stray thought she had had during the evening. Could it be some form of amnesia that ailed the boy? He never mentioned his family. What if he had been told what his name was yet did not really "know" it? Simon had never answered her question about an illness.

Ought she to meddle? She said to herself, *Nonsense. How can it do anything but good to eat some decent meals at regular hours and have a place to stay for a few nights, and a little peace? That couldn't hurt him or anyone in the world!*

Or could it?

But Mrs. Moffat refused to think about that possibility. She did not know then that it was a very definite possibility—part of a very definite plan. . . .

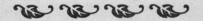

The Protégé

by Charlotte Armstrong

A FAWCETT CREST BOOK

Fawcett Publications, Inc., Greenwich, Conn.

THE PROTÉGÉ

Chapter 1

WHEN Mrs. Moffat—aware that someone had been ushered into the pew from the side aisle and had skinned past two pairs of knees and then a bare patch to settle beside her—turned to send a Sunday smile to whatever seeker, the startling young person said, "Good morning, Mrs. Moffat."

"Well! Good morning!" She was surprised; but the choir was coming in, and, on her feet for the introit, she had time to wonder whose child this was and whether she ought to have recognized him. By the time the congregation was released to sit down after the invocation she had decided rather crossly, No, because *this* child, following fashion, was wearing a full beard and a mustache. Mrs. Moffat did not care for whiskers. "They all peer at you nowadays," she said to herself, "over unsanitary muffs." Yet she already knew that this one was different.

He was reaching for the hymnal; the skin of his hand was tanned and slightly freckled, but so clean as to seem to shine. She took a sideways glance at that head and what could be seen of the face. The nose was straight, neither long nor short, nothing distinguished. But the hair, helmeting the round skull, masking the cheeks, the chin, obscuring the lines of the lips, was red. Not literally red, of course, and not the true orange that is called "red" hair, but a shining and glowing auburn. Very clean, tightly curled, cropped close, it was like astrakhan. She'd had a baby-lamb coat, once . . .

He was dressed in a brown suit, clean and in press, but not a fine fabric. He had put something down on the floor on his other side. She didn't think she had seen him before in her life.

She thought, *He could have come off a stained-glass*

window! and then, *What is he doing in* church, *for heaven's sake?*

They stood to sing. Taller than she, he was not very tall, stocky in the bone, thin in the flesh. Mrs. Moffat accepted her half of the hymnal. A very slight tremor was transmitted across the book's spine. Mrs. Moffat wasn't sure which one of them was trembling.

The boy, the young man (*How* young? Everybody— Presidents, Senators, savants, and philosophers—looked young to Mrs. Moffat these days) did not try to sing. He seemed, in a dreamy way, to be listening.

So Mrs. Moffat, who had once been able to sing, at least in the parlor, found herself singing now as well as she possibly could.

As they settled down again, she had only one thing more to whisper. "Is my cane bothering you?" It was lying on the pew bench in the very angle of seat and back.

"Oh, no, Mrs. Moffat," he said, low-voiced. His lashes were auburn.

All the way through the service Mrs. Moffat could not help feeling accompanied or perhaps followed. He listened as gravely as she to the anthem. When she took out her envelope, he put a dollar bill in an envelope from the tiny rack and dropped it on the plate with the same casual air as she. He sat as patiently and impatiently as she during the sermon, which fell, as usual, to sink without a bounce, into the plush of the "proper" resolutions of the pious not to betray by any sound or sign that anything said meant anything at all to any one of them. Mrs. Moffat fumed gently to herself and, when it was over, sighed. The boy ducked his head as if he had caught himself about to sigh.

They rose for the benediction. Then it was time to nod to acquaintances. Mrs. Moffat saw Crystal and Claire going out the far side door. They had not seen her. She was just as glad. She would skip the line of handshakers before the minister, too, she decided. She didn't know how to explain this young man, whoever he was, who preceded her along the aisle, nodding to no one, but in some subtle manner making a way for her alone.

They emerged into California sunshine. As Mrs. Moffat began to feel with her cane for the brink of the six stone steps she had come to dread, the young man moved into a position almost directly in front of her, but two steps lower. "Could you use my shoulder, Mrs. Moffat?" She was pleased. Yes, she was! Using her cane with her left hand, she put her right hand on his shoulder, and with his strength and his balance at her disposal she tripped down the perilous way with wonderful ease. That was imaginative! she thought. How she did dread being seized under one wing by some male who thought he was being gallant, but who inevitably destroyed her own balance at once, so that if her feet were to go all the way from under her, she would be bound to dangle lopsidedly helpless, and her escort unable to do a thing about it except dump her in a ludicrous heap and start all over again.

So, safely arrived at level ground, she looked up to thank him sincerely. The sharp summer sunlight must be harsh on her ancient face, but Marguerite Moffat still knew how to send out through her eyes the sparkle of her spirit, provided anyone was looking for it.

"I guess you don't remember, ma'am," he said. His voice was soft and had a pleasant grain to it. She could see his eyes now. They were amber and had, of themselves, a certain—placidity, was it? Opacity? A touch of *qué será será?* "Simon Warren?" he said, and listened as if he had thrown a stone and waited for the ripple to widen.

"Warren?" She couldn't remember any . . .

"The Warrens that used to live next door to you, a long time ago?"

"Oh," she said, pleased to be enlightened. "Well! Simon Warren! Of course I remember, but it's been years!"

"Yes, ma'am." He was watching her, as if he were testing?

Mrs. Moffat took refuge in the truth. "I remember you as being twelve or thirteen years old when you moved away," she said. "I certainly wouldn't have known you today. Why, you must be"—*He's the very same age as Tommy*, she thought with a pang—"twenty-eight, isn't it?"

"Yes, I guess so, ma'am."

"And how are your folks?" she inquired cordially. Mrs. Moffat was aware of covert glances from the throng. "Who *is* that, with Mrs. Moffat?" "Who *is* that, with the old lady in the pink hat?" His looks were sufficiently startling anywhere and, in this place, uncanny.

"Just fine, I guess," he was answering. "I haven't seen them for quite a while." He had, she noticed now, one of those canvas bags that airlines give you, in his left hand. He stood passively.

"What are you doing here, Simon?" she inquired, beginning to move along.

He fell in beside her, moved with her at her pace. "Oh, I just thought I'd come by . . ."

"Revisiting the scenes of your youth, eh?" said Mrs. Moffat. "You used to walk to Sunday school. Have you been to see your old house?"

"Not yet . . ."

"Then why don't you ride along with me?"

"Why, I'd sure like to, ma'am. Thank you."

Mrs. Moffat took the way to the parking lot, and if any eyebrows wanted to wag in her wake, let them. Although she was seventy-four years old, she still had her driver's license and drove herself short distances around town. The boy opened the car's door and saw her in, but he did not try to "help" her. (Oh, the "kind" people who lifted and tugged and made her much more helpless than she needed to be!) Mrs. Moffat got in smoothly, with well-practiced movements, wondering fleetingly at the boy's unusual manners. Her erstwhile neighbors had never impressed her as the kind of people to teach such non-mechanical thoughtfulness to a son whom she now remembered to have been a perfectly normal and impudent rapscallion.

"How have you been, Simon?" she asked as he got in beside her. "Put your bag in the back if you like. On the wing, are you?"

"I've been back on the mainland for a little while," he said stolidly.

(Mainland? Ah, one picked that up in the islands.) "In the service?" she guessed.

"Yes, ma'am." He didn't volunteer which branch. "I've been out of it awhile."

"Long enough to grow a stylish beard, I see," she teased. She turned the car into the street, thinking he wouldn't look so darned Biblical if he'd just shave.

"On your way home, I suppose?" she continued. "Are your folks still living in Pennsylvania? Your mother used to send me Christmas cards, but they've died down."

He didn't respond.

"What are you going to do with yourself now that you're out?" she continued amiably. This is what you did with the young. You asked them all the old expected questions, so as not to frighten them.

"I'm not going home," he said. "I can't say what I'm going to do." He squirmed a little, as if he didn't like the old expected questions; he didn't have the expected answers?

She started to ask how long he'd been away from the mainland, but then did not. "I suppose it all seems strange," she said instead.

"It sure does," he said gratefully. "It doesn't look really real to *me*, Mrs. Moffat. I don't really recognize anything."

"I can imagine," she said soothingly, not at all sure that this was true.

She wondered how he had been able to recognize *her*. Ah, well, once a woman succumbs to being an old woman, she changes very slowly thereafter. Mrs. Moffat would have been fifty-seven, pushing sixty, that summer when this boy and her grandson, Tommy, had been eleven. *Yes*, she thought, remembering that season, *I must have succumbed just about then*.

"This is a nice car," he said shyly but with what sounded like genuine pleasure. "It's sure green and pretty here. It's probably changed."

The car was five years old, but unblemished. Mrs.

Moffat always drove it sedately along accustomed rounds. The neighborhood was pretty, a backwater along the Arroyo Seco, old trees, old lawns, old houses, nothing spectacular. To her it had not changed much. *Backwaters are like old women,* she thought. She told him so, thinking, *He's changed. Places revisited will let you know that. Well, God knows what he's seen.*

She didn't ask him whether he had been, for instance, wounded. Or wounded in his mind by horrors. In either case Mrs. Moffat didn't want the details, nor would he wish to dwell on them. She surmised that he was feeling somewhat numb. Lost, perhaps? Confused? Seeking backward for a place to put an emotional foot? Well, she couldn't guide him.

He said, seeming to rouse himself as if to duty, "Tommy Moffat—I mean your Tommy—he and I used to play. Do you remember?"

"I remember," she said. Then, forgetting, as old women do, that she had not spoken all her thoughts aloud, she added tartly, "You don't want to talk about some things."

"Pardon?" He was startled. He turned his head, and his right hand flew to the fur on his chin.

Mrs. Moffat kept her eyes on the street. "I understand," she said, "because some things I prefer not to discuss either. So we'll not talk about Tommy Moffat. Okay?"

"Okay," he echoed feebly.

"I see no particular virtue in hashing over old sins and old sorrows," said Mrs. Moffat severely. "For one thing, I haven't got the time."

He made no response. In a little while she knew his head was turned very slightly toward her and his pupils had slid to the very left-hand corners of his eyes so that he could study her.

Mrs. Moffat, who was not without at least some glinting contacts with modern youth, thought to herself, *Well, if he grew that beard to be in style, he didn't make it. He suspects I'm alive. He's not in style.*

The street, curving along the gully, was lined with

houses only on their left. Mrs. Moffat's dwelling stood on a fair-sized plot of ground, and scaled against the great trees on either side, it seemed to be a small two-story clapboard under a steep roof, the walls painted white, with hints of gingerbread. But since it trailed off into a one-story extension at the back, it was much more spacious than could be guessed from the street.

Mrs. Moffat made the car hesitate opposite the green stucco on the near side of her own place. "There you are," she said. "I forget what color it was in your mother's day. It's been green ever since the Hallorans bought it. Do you know, Simon, I've just remembered they are in Europe? But I don't see why you couldn't walk around the yard if you like. Let me pull into my driveway."

The boy said nothing; he gazed almost sleepily the way she had been pointing.

She swooped around into her driveway, which passed her dining room and kitchen, on the far right of her property and continued into the back regions where her detached garage was set deep into the plot and was yet only halfway to the inner boundary. Mrs. Moffat drove into the garage, at its center, leaving wide margins on each side. (Only one car to fit in now.) The boy was out quickly and opening her door. She said decisively, "Why don't you prowl around as much as you like?" She walked into the open, and he followed. "Afterward maybe you would take a bite of lunch with me?"

He said mechanically, "Oh, no, thank you, ma'am. It would be too much bother—"

Mrs. Moffat was having none of that. "I wouldn't ask you if it was going to be a bother," she announced. "I don't mean Sunday *dinner*. It'll be a bite, as I said, and we'll take it on my back porch, as I usually do, picnic-style. Polly (you must remember Polly) will enjoy the whole thing very much."

Mrs. Moffat wasn't waiting for his consent. She proceeded briskly along the gravel path to the house, passing the mouth of the short path to the house, passing the mouth of the short path to the wing of her garage, passing the clump of shrubbery that made that part a tunnel.

Then, missing the crunch of his following feet, she stopped and turned.

He was gazing across her grassy domain. "There's the sundial," he said in a breathless way.

Mrs. Moffat looked at him, her eyebrows drawing together. He seemed delighted. She caught the impact of her own familiar place with the freshness of his sudden sight of it. Her lawns seemed vast, rolling upward ever so slightly as they did, leading the eye to the evergreen mass of the tall back hedge. She grew very few flowers any more, but the oleanders were sprinkling the shrubbery with white or bright pink, and this was pleasant. The thick green of the ivy ground cover, edging the borders, scalloped the whole, and here and there a band of gray dusty millers marked one of the curves very handsomely.

In full summer the air was crisp and dry and hot. The sun was high. Her huge black acacia stood in a puddle of shade, tight to its trunk. The sundial was out from under the huge tree now. How that tree alone must have grown, she thought, in fifteen years.

"Things have changed some," she said lightly. "The trees and I are older, for one thing. You can go around by the sidewalk, Simon. Or, if you remember the place where you used to skin through the hedge, you can try, although it may be grown over. Then come back and join me, do."

"Yes, ma'am," he said dreamily.

So she nodded to indicate an understanding and went on toward the wide back porch, an old-fashioned feature screened all around and furnished without benefit of plastic, which Mrs. Moffat much enjoyed and stubbornly refused to call a patio. As she opened the screen door, she noticed that Simon Warren, walking on her driveway, had chosen to go by way of the sidewalk.

Polly Kroenke, spotless in the blue and white she always wore (pale blue for summer, navy for winter), came to be told who that was, exclaimed over the news, and trotted off to the kitchen, joyously rising to the challenge, as Mrs. Moffat had known she would.

Herself, she went into her huge sitting room, so cool

and dim, where she took off her pink hat, her short pink gloves, and set them with her pink church pocketbook on a table corner.

She sighed and left off wondering (as she often did) whatever she would do without Polly, who had kept her house for forty years and still kept it. It was hard to believe that Polly was sixty-two; she moved so spryly in the familiar patterns. She had a long face and cheeks of a curious flatness, with long grooves in them now. She wore her hair flat on the top, in a style she had never changed. Polly had not changed very much. Mrs. Moffat still must keep a firm rein on an inclination to fuss and overdo. Polly was not a companion in the sense that the two of them could exchange very much in the way of informed opinion. *But a housemate, all the same, so long as we both shall live,* thought Mrs. Moffat. *It was too late now for Polly to have another kind of life, and mine has come to stagnant peace,* she thought. Ah, well, worse things could happen.

The lady of the house was feeling a bit exhausted. The energy aroused by surprise was fading. She regretted, slightly at least, that she had asked Simon Warren to lunch, but she really could not have sent the lad away at mealtime. It was too late to abandon some ingrained habits of hospitality. Oh, well, she would acquire merit, at least in the eyes of a woman with whom she had once been neighborly, and perhaps, thought Mrs. Moffat, in the eyes of the Lord, although by definition she couldn't fool Him.

She sat down in her pet chair and caused it to recline. This long room was clean in effect. She knew better about the corners. It was orderly. Who was to litter it? It was very seldom that any children came. The decor was old-fashioned (Zan always said so). *But then,* thought Mrs. Moffat, *I am old-fashioned, and everything here is mine, so it is as it should be.* She put her head back and mused in peace. At least Simon Warren had not turned out to be one of the current crop who thought that rudeness and filth signified an *advance*. She had sensed nothing aggressive or hostile either. But if not, why not? she wondered.

He must be tired, she concluded—weary and worn down to some residue of ingrained courtesy, that which had both astonished and pleased her. He did seem thin for the size of his bones. Somebody ought to feed him well, fatten him up . . .

Mrs. Moffat dealt briefly with the stirrings of temptation, and having skillfully dismissed them, she slipped easily into a catnap.

She woke when she heard Polly exclaiming, "Well! Simon Warren! Well! Come in, come in."

The boy said, "Mrs. Moffat asked me to come back," as if he weren't sure he ought to believe it.

Mrs. Moffat brought her chair upright, wiggled out of it, instantly alert, by no means disheveled. Her pink dress was a "miracle" fabric. It couldn't wrinkle. She wore her scant gray hair in a knot on the top of her head (which was neat and stayed neat and got it out of her way). Cosmetics had failed her long ago. She walked on her small neat feet, in the pink but sensible flats, out to the porch. "Come in," she said to the boy, who hesitated. "You've remembered Polly? Hasn't he grown, eh, Polly? Sit down, Simon. Well? What did you think? I'm sorry you won't get to see the inside. But they've made changes, you know. It wouldn't be the same."

"No," he said serenely. "Nothing's going to be the same. I don't mind not getting to see the inside."

Mrs. Moffat sat down, noticing that he was not going to do so until she was settled. This pleased her. "Would you like something cold to drink now? Beer, for instance?" (Boys like beer.) "We have some beer, don't we, Polly?" Mrs. Moffat kept it for Joe when Joe and Flo came.

"Oh, yes, Mrs. Moffat."

"*I'm* going to have some beer," said Mrs. Moffat firmly. "Sit down, sit down."

"Then I'd sure like some," her guest said promptly. Polly beamed and bustled away. The boy chose one of the rockers and surrendered to it. He was gazing out at the many greens, the green-gold where the sun bounced, the deep-green in the low shadow, and a hundred greens in between. "It's just like a park," he said softly. "Your own park—and hidden all around."

"I suppose it is," she said. "Everything's grown so high. And it's all mine, that's true. My husband—Mr. Moffat—died"—Mrs. Moffat would not say "passed away"—"ten years ago, Simon. You may have heard."

"Yes, ma'am," he said gravely.

She went on. "It must be forty-five years ago that he built this house." (Thomas, the son, had been seven.) "So," she said, "all this is mine, as he arranged for it to be. And so long as I have Polly to look after me, here I stay. The fact is," she added, as she had not meant to add aloud, "I really wouldn't know where in the whole world else to go."

The boy had set his rocking chair to moving slightly. *Why isn't he either too young or not young enough,* she asked herself suddenly, *to fall so easily into a cradle rhythm?* But she went on chattering, since she seemed to know her voice was soothing to him. Perhaps it was only that as long as she kept talking he need not? "You may conclude that I am lonely," she said, betraying herself blithely to this not necessarily attentive but patient listener. "The few of my old friends who still survive are enough. Enough. I can't take crowds anymore. And big social doings. I expect I've 'dropped out,' if the truth were known. Oh, I have young Alexandra, that's my granddaughter. We call her Zan. She comes every summer to visit, and while she's here, she bosses me around, and that's amusing while it lasts. You don't want to hear the story of my life," Mrs. Moffat said cheerfully. (Simon could have been dozing with his eyes open.) "Still— when you've got to the last chapter," she went on, "and there's not going to be much *plot* to the rest of it, you tend to keep on summing up. My life was interesting to me"—she smiled—"and maybe, when I get to heaven, they'll supply some angel who'll be dying to hear all about it. I can wait," she added merrily. "Ah, the beer."

He thanked Polly in the nice shy way he had. He lifted the glass and sipped. Mrs. Moffat kept still, feeling foolish. *Ah, well,* she thought crossly, *let him listen to the old lady. It's like singing for his supper in reverse. That's fair enough, surely.*

The cold liquid seemed to be bringing his brown eyes to life. He said, "I'll tell you what it seems like here to me, Mrs. Moffat. It seems to me like you've already got to heaven."

She was so touched that her eyes swam. Her hand trembled. Her glass tilted. She set it down quickly and dabbed at the bosom of her dress.

Then the boy was asking softly where he could go to wash.

So Mrs. Moffat sent him to Polly to be shown to the downstairs lavatory. She was a little upset. It didn't *do* to be pierced so suddenly by something akin to sadness, yet akin to joy.

When he came back, shining, she embarked on an analysis of the sermon; this was, after all, an experience in the present tense that they had had in common. He didn't contribute. He hadn't really paid that much attention, he now confessed, but she made him laugh a time or two . . . and Mrs. Moffat had again to curb her tongue and dampen down her spirits and remember what she would probably have to pay for having so much fun as this.

But after they had eaten the cold and tasty fare and Polly had whisked away the dishes, Mrs. Moffat felt herself begin to droop. She hunted for a kindly way to indicate that the festivities were over. She asked if Simon would like to walk around the grounds with her, a tour she was accustomed to take at least once a day, for the air and the delicate exercise. She often walked, she told him, just before she took her afternoon rest.

So she led him through the house, through the big sitting room, to the little square hall from which the stairs went up, past the arch to the parlor (never used), and Gerard's den opposite, and out the front and around to the right, and down the side path on the north side along which the camellias grew—now ten feet high—and then to the oval of lawn in which the sundial was centered nowadays.

Simon was again bemused to see it

"It counts only sunny hours," Mrs. Moffat said somewhat derisively. "And that's right, Simon. It won't give you the time of night, I can tell you that. It's obsolete. It can't cope, anyhow. Daylight saving has addled its wits, poor ancient thing."

He said, "Didn't it used to have a ring of flowers?"

"Why, yes," she said, startled for some reason. "Now ... here," she went on, rounding the peninsula of shrubs and coming to the second bay of lawn on this side, "is where my son used to have his playground when he was a little boy. Oh, you never knew my son. He had gone away from here before you were born. You would have been only three years old when Thomas died. I only had the one child. He was never—robust."

There she went again, telling the story of her life. She looked at him sharply.

He was gazing at the ground. He said, "I guess people die."

And again he had pleased her. She said, feeling released, "He was only twenty-nine. Only a year older than you are now. You wouldn't think that was much of a life. But I guess we shouldn't be so sure. Time"—she was thinking aloud again—"is not the same for different people. For me, time's been slow, flowing along, you know ... but on the whole more like a lake than a river. For some, I suppose, it's wild and deep and they live twice as fast—or twice as much." She swayed with momentary dizziness.

He did not step to steady her. He said, "Mrs. Moffat, I might have had my life, for all I know."

Mrs. Moffat thought, *I don't want to hear about his troubles.*

"Look!" she said. "There! See? Where the branch is bouncing? Look at him watching us, the rascal! A squirrel!"

"I see."

The sun shone on the bright color of Simon's beard. She was beginning to be able to see his face in spite of it. He seemed rapt. He seemed very, very young.

"What do you suppose a squirrel makes of human

beings?" said Mrs. Moffat. "I often wonder. Does he know we are watching him? Can *he* conceive of eyes?"

"I never thought of that," the boy said, as if he were delighted. "But he knows! He's got to know, ma'am. Maybe he can't conceive of eyes, but he *knows* he's being seen." His eyebrows drew together and knotted. "Isn't that wonderful?" he said, rather dully.

"Yes, it is," said Mrs. Moffat in a matter-of-fact way. She was somewhat surprised by his response, but willing to accept it. "Come along," she continued, "I always go all the way up to the end, and then we'll turn down the other side."

But she was tired now and fell silent. Gerard had instituted this patrol. Mornings and evenings he had gone this way, to see what the flowers were up to. But the flowers were gone, and so was he; only the habit remained.

"What is *that*, ma'am?" Simon stopped to stare at the wing that angled away from the garage.

"Oh, you remember," she said, cross with fatigue. "We call it the cottage, although it's no such thing. Just a room and bath and a teensy kitchenette. Mr. McGregor used to live there, in the old days. Had he gone when you were living next door? I don't think so. You must have known old Mr. McGregor, who took care of the gardens then? We had such flowers. My husband liked to watch them bud and bloom and fade, but he hadn't the slightest idea how to grow them. Mr. McGregor had a very green thumb. He used to grow tomatoes for the table. Nobody else could, for miles around. Now, of course, I just have Ben Guest, who comes once a week and mows and clips and keeps the jungle from swallowing me up. Oh, don't look in!" Simon was peering in at the dirty window. "I'm ashamed," she said. "It's not used anymore, and we've let it go. Ben never does find the time to clean it out, you see, and it's too much for Polly and me. Come along," she said, distressed for some reason.

He turned his head. She had not seen his eyes lit from the inside except once—in connection with the squirrel.

"I'll clean it for you," he said. "Let me do it."

"No, no. It's a terrible job! You don't want—"

"Yes, I do," he insisted. "If I could find a broom ... and if there's water and soap, and a mop, or something. Please?"

"You don't mean *now?*"

"Could I? Please!"

"Well," she said, "it's not that I think there's anything wrong about cleaning up on Sunday ... but ... I don't know what I could pay ... and you'd get yourself so messy." (*He doesn't like that*, she thought shrewdly, bent on dissuading him.)

"Oh, not for pay!" he cried. "Not for pay. I've got some work clothes with me." He was very tense. "You'd rather it was clean, wouldn't you? Please?"

Mrs. Moffat knew that she ought to say a very firm No and walk on. But she couldn't at the moment think *why* this was so. She took refuge in as much of the truth as she was sure of and said, "Oh, I would rather it was clean. No doubt of that, but—"

He took this for consent. His teeth flashed. He began to run. He ran round to the garage ... ran to find his work pants.

Somewhat ruffled and dismayed, Mrs. Moffat made her way to the cottage door. It wasn't locked. The key had been lost years ago. She opened the door and looked in with loathing at the layers of dust, the gardener's muddy tracks across the worn old rug, the sagging bedstead, the limp and dirty curtains. "Well," she said, as the boy came racing in, his bag in his hand, "this is a disgrace! The plumbing is all right. The bathroom's in operation. Ben uses it, I'm happy to see. But there's no hot water. The gas was turned off long ago."

The boy, scarcely listening, was bristling with energy, only wanting to get on with it. So Mrs. Moffat who could have even now said No did not. She could not. It seemed too cruel.

"I'll see whether Polly can find you some things to use," she promised, and walked slowly on the hot green grass back to the house.

Chapter 2

ALL Sunday afternoon Mrs. Moffat sat on the porch, reaping the whirlwind. She couldn't go up to her room in the front of the house to rest, with all this going on. Polly, armed with pails and mops and brooms and rags and brushes, had joined the fray. Her mistress had no doubt but that Polly was having the time of her life.

Mrs. Moffat was and was not enjoying what she could see of the battle. Sometimes she felt just a trifle hurt to have been left out of it. But she was cast as audience, spectator, patron-to-be-pleased, goddess, or victim. She sat in her favorite rocker; sometimes she had to chuckle. She was watching, as it were, an explosion that was taking place just out of sight. The clump of shrubs hid the cottage door. Even so she seemed to see things bursting out of that door. The raggedy curtains sailed over the flowering pomegranate bush. Then Simon, naked to the waist (tan, but so thin), came out of the path's tunnel, dragging the old rug to the driveway, where he beat it and shook it, and the clouds that rose were mortifying. But the scene was funny in a way. Oh, the furious two-legged creature against the dust that was immortal!

Another time the mattress walked into view, the boy invisible behind it. He dropped the mattress on the grass; he swept it and beat it on both sides. When he left it healing in the sun, this pleased her.

Then he had the garden hose. What was he doing with the garden hose? She heard the roar of water fanning hard into a pail. So Mrs. Moffat was both entertained and uneasy. All the while, over her head, she knew (she knew!) a hand was writing on a wall.

Polly came to the porch at last, streaked and panting. "Oh, look at me," she cried. "Oh, *I* got to get cleaned up!

Oh, he's not missing a thing, Mrs. Moffat. Wait till you see. But he don't want you coming out there till he's got hisself cleaned up. So you just wait. You wait!" Polly went joyously staggering off to her first-floor room.

Mrs. Moffat rocked and contemplated the moment that was coming, a moment she had never thought to live through again. The moment known to all women who have ever born a child. The moment one's child will say, "Mother, Mother, come see what *I* did!" And Mother goes, to crown achievement with justice and mercy, goddess and slave.

In a while the boy came, calm and immaculate, all eagerness invisible. So Mrs. Moffat went, walking in as much dignity as she could, at five feet two and round in the middle.

It was a squarish room, and fair-sized, with opposite sides to the weather. Its furnishings were shabby, of course. They were the castoffs of years. But all fabrics had been brushed, brightened. All wood surfaces polished. The windowpanes were bare, but bright. He seemed to have actually washed the walls down. The floor had been scrubbed. The old rug had had the decency to revive and show some color. The bed was spread; he had squared it and braced it.

Mrs. Moffat was able to exclaim in genuine wonder, and she was glad, because she didn't think she could have fooled him. Not about cleanliness. (He was somewhat obsessed by that, was he not? Was this a *good* sign?) But truly she had not remembered that the cottage could be so—well—attractive. She said so. Proudly (he *was* proud, wasn't that it?) he showed her the inside of the tiny clothes closet, which was spotless. He showed her the very small bath at the end of the room. It had no tub, only a shower. All the fixtures were shining. He had brushed down and somehow polished the bamboo curtain that hung as a partition before the alcove kitchenette next to the bath. But now he apologized. He had not got around to the kitchen. There was an awful lot to do in there. "The stove is rusty, and that's going to take hard scraping. Could I come back and do it tomorrow?" he asked her in eager innocence.

Yes—innocence. Mrs. Moffat was shocked. He wasn't hinting. He wasn't being sly. He wasn't even imagining? No, she was sure of it. But how was it possible that the inevitable had not even crossed his mind, the thing that was written on the wall?

She said slowly, "Simon, where do you plan to spend the night?"

"Oh," he said indifferently, "I don't know, ma'am. I'll find some room. It doesn't matter."

"Would you like to stay here, in the cottage?"

The lines on the lower half of his face remained masked. But she watched in his eyes the dawning intelligence. He said, "That's why I just *had* to do this? Do you think so?"

"I don't know," she said quietly. "Is it?"

He stood in the middle of the floor. He had lowered his head, that odd astrakhan head. He said, "I *made* you ask me?"

"The fact is," she said, her sharp old voice dispelling mists, "I *have* asked you, so if you're willing to risk the presence of some uprooted spider who's bound to resent that, you are welcome. Now rest," she cried. "For heaven's sake, lie down a little bit before it's suppertime."

He raised his head and said, "I sure would like to stay here, Mrs. Moffat. To me, it's perfect. But I'll go and get me a hamburger somewhere, if you don't mind. I don't mind. I don't want you to feed me *again*. At least, not now."

Mrs. Moffat thought she could understand how he felt. It didn't do to take too much. It didn't do. There was always a turning against too much to be grateful for. It put you off your balance, and that doesn't do—unless you cannot help it.

"Just as you'd rather," she said kindly. "Go and find yourself some supper then. Not that Polly doesn't always fix too much for me. Will you try to believe that before breakfast?"

She would have touched him lightly, to indicate, as it

was her impulse to do, that her bounty was lightly given.
But he swayed away. He was looking at her with an odd
glow in his eyes. She could scarcely believe her intuition
that it was a genuine curiosity, a look that wondered.
Now what kind of person is this I am seeing before me?

She smiled and cocked her head and said, "You're
welcome," as if he'd thanked her, as perhaps he had. She
walked out of the cottage and slowly back to the house.
What have I done? she wondered.

She told Polly what she had done. Polly began to beam
and talk about what bedding they could spare.

"Take him what he needs," said Mrs. Moffat wearily.
"There's plenty." She went to her sitting room, turned on
her TV, and sat down. *Well, Polly's an old fool, too,* she
thought grimly. *How do we know he's not going off to
summon a gang, now that he's sure we are two old
crones, alone here?*

She punched her remote control irritably, changing
channels. She was just too old to be afraid of gangs and
robbers. It wasn't really real, this kind of fear. She and
Polly would lock the doors and the downstairs windows
as they always did. The phone was, as ever, at her bed-
side. Why, if she wanted to, Mrs. Moffat could even arm
herself. There was a gun in the house. Her husband had
kept it by him for years. She'd been taught to use it. She
never had. She wasn't sure how clean it was, but she
didn't doubt it constituted a weapon. *An equalizer,* she
thought grumpily.

At least she hadn't been reckless enough to offer him
one of the indoor guest rooms.

She then seemed to know that Simon Warren might not
have accepted such an offer. It was the cottage, shabby
but adequate, and "hidden all around," that was "perfect" for him.

The thick lead of the stubby pencil came off in wide
strokes on the notebook paper.

DEAR SMITTY:
     Hell, it was easy. I ask the usher. "Right down there, in the
pink hat," he says, and then he takes me right down there. So

I ride home with her. How do you like that? She's rich, all right, but I don't know—she doesn't make a big deal out of—

The pencil hesitated; then it blackened out the last line. The hand pushed the notebook away and positioned the cheap envelope. P. H. ALLENSTAG, JR. the pencil wrote. His hand turned over, back to the table, fingers lax. The waiter came with a plate on which a mound of pale french fried potatoes obscured everything else. The boy with the red beard picked up the notebook, but the envelope he pushed to his left, placing the written name where it could be easily read. Then, chin to chest, he twisted his neck far as it could twist and looked up slyly to watch the waiter's face. The waiter put the plate down and went away.

Alexandra Terry, looking out her window at some Manhattan towers, said into the telephone, "Nicky? Zan here. I've got a question."

"Ask me anything," said Nicholas Pomerance, looking out at his smog-smudged view of the sprawl of Los Angeles, "but tell me how you are."

"Will you be around, come the tenth of August, and for a fortnight thereafter? And I'm fine."

"Ah," said he, "we are threatening our annual pilgrimage, are we?"

"We are," said Zan. "I'd like to know whether I will have a squire during that span. You see, if it turns out I'd rather choose another time—"

"Any time, Zan. Any time. I'm doing business at the old grindstone. Took my vacation in June, fool that I was."

"And where did you go in June?"

"Ahunting."

"Ahunting what?"

"Birds. What else? Beware the playboy image, Zan, when I, like any other trapped and salaried male, go my dreary rounds with only the slightest interludes for dalliance."

"Ah, so," she said, grinning to herself over an image of his bland and sometimes deceptively foolish-looking face.

Nicky cast a glance toward the two lovelies in his kitchen, who were discussing the mystique of the omelet and disputing procedures. Nicky didn't trust them. *He* was going to make the omelet.

"By the way," he said, "how is my sister?"

"The complete suburban housewife," said Zan. "Four wee hands tugging at her apron strings already, and the rumor of two more come spring. Didn't you know?"

Nicky groaned. "Well, Jane does tend to be thorough."

Zan didn't speak, and he said alertly, "Anything else I ought to know?"

"Oh, there's a spot of other news, such as it is. I went to the law. I am now legally a widow."

"What does that mean?" he asked suspiciously. "You've got reason to start in to worry about, for instance, Enoch Arden?"

"No, no," said Zan. "But it's seven years since Tommy Moffat took off. So it was the *classic* thing, wasn't it? I just came all over sensible, I guess."

"Oh, surely not," drawled Nicky, "more sensible than usual? You *are* going to be sensible and stay with your grandmother?"

"Of course."

"How is the old lady?" Nicky asked smoothly. "All right, isn't she?" Over the phone, Zan sent the image of widened eyes.

"Okay, so I should have gone to see her . . ."

"Don't worry about it." Zan forgave him for nothing. "The last thing Gran expects is a gentleman caller. But I can rely on you, can't I?"

"I'll make it a point to meet your plane. How's that for a reckless offer?"

She gave him the day—Monday—and the flight number.

"You're not by any chance taking a one-way ticket this time?" he inquired with a wheedling air.

"Is this not a reckless question, Nicky?"

"No, no, certainly not. I can be almost as sensible as you. Wanna bet?"

"I'm thinking," she admitted.

"No harm in that," said he.

Zan hung up smiling. Nicky amused her, and she was fond of him. If she had not confided her true motives in the matter of going to the law, why should she? Now that Zan had prospered and had her own money in the bank, she had had the bitter thought that it was wise to protect herself. Tommy Moffat was just the type to pick up the scent of money, however far away he might (or might not) be. And it was not only Zan's earned money, but old Mrs. Moffat's estate, too. Zan was the heir. It had all been willed to her, and Tommy specifically disinherited and cause given that no probate court could ignore. But some-one had pointed out to Zan that if Tommy could prove himself to be still legally her husband—then there might be trouble. Zan, for a long time, had had her guard up against any more trouble than she had already seen. So, although it had upset her (irrationally) to have Tommy declared legally dead, for all she knew he *was* dead, and if not, it was better to have on record somewhere the whole story from Zan's point of view.

She began to roam restlessly through her rooms. They were perfect, absolutely perfect. She had decorated them herself and showed them off from time to time to confirm, or inform, that she had her skills. But now they bored her. Everything here was exactly as she thought it ought to be, and she was perishing of something like frustration.

Zan was twenty-five years old, slender, with good taut lines to her figure, and a pretty face, distinguished by a mouth that might have been ugly since it was set, full-lipped, forward of her cheeks, but that by virtue of this defect, was very attractive. She was her own woman, or almost. She wore what she liked, trusting her taste. She had energy and verve. She was succeeding; better than that, she had learned a lot. She had done very well.

To have become a junior partner in a going concern at Zan's age was an achievement not to be despised. But the texture of life had more to it than status or financial gain. Her senior—Grace Bond, of Bond & Terry, Interiors—had begun, since the partnership, to emanate certain rays

that Zan didn't want to think about. She couldn't be sure
what they were, but the one sure way not to have to think
about what they might be was to pull out and move, for
instance, to the coast.

Zan sat down and began to add up the pros and cons
for Southern California.

It would be risky to start all over again and on her own
in a new town. She wouldn't mind that; on the contrary,
what sport!

She would also be living closer to old Mrs. Moffat and
better able to watch over her, so dangerously aged and
alone in that big old house—alone, that is, with Polly,
who was not, in Zan's opinion, the brightest person in the
world. There was no use pretending that the old lady was
going to live forever, and it wasn't sensible not to be
conscious of the fact that when the inevitable did happen,
Zan would, at that time, be forced to hop it out there and
remain a good deal longer than it took to hold a decent
funeral, too. There was the property to deal with, and
Zan had to do it. She didn't *need* the property; silly to
pretend it wouldn't be interesting to have it. Zan wasn't
afraid to think these thoughts because she was sure of
her own sincere hope that death would hold off for a good
while yet. She was very fond of her husband's grandmother, who had stood by Zan during the most difficult period
of her entire life. (Zan had no intention of going through
anything any *worse*. Not if she could help it.) Well, then,
she could keep a closer eye on Gran ... and *say* she was
keeping an eye on her legacy, which would make a mar-
velous excuse for getting out of her present commitments
without argument. Everybody respected a money motive.
Such was the virtue of a cliché.

Now then, she mused on, once out there, she might or
she might not marry Nicky Pomerance. His sister, Jane,
who had been Zan's buddy in college, had once insisted
that they look each other up. Zan had known him a long
time. Three, almost four years now? Nicky was thirty-
five—a sensible age—and he was no unknown quantity.
He was a burned child, just as she was. His divorce had
been a painful enough experience to keep Nicky from

being romantically carried away on any future occasion. And Zan, having survived her own crisis, was never again going to be taken in by moonlight and roses. It might work out rather well.

But she stopped herself from adding up the pros and cons of a marriage to Nicky. There wasn't enough evidence in. How reliable was their personal compatibility? Would their two careers be compatible at all?

And where was the gain?

Zan had no desire to get married for the sake of getting married. To live with a cheater and be a cheat herself didn't seem worth the price of the wedding costumes. (As for champagne, that was available at any time.) And children, Zan didn't think about—anymore.

Well, she would scout out many prospects on the coast this visit. How she could start herself in a new phase of her career, what strings she might have to pull, what security there was in the way of paying jobs, in case her private enterprise should fail.

But then she ran her fingers through her very short dark hair and held her skull, her bone tightly. Thinking. Thinking. She'd burst someday of thinking. Zan knew how to get what she wanted—with intelligence, industry, persistence, and plan—but how did you get what you really wanted when intelligence, industry, persistence, and plan had nothing to do with it?

Chapter 3

MONDAY was another clear hot day. When Mrs. Moffat came down, Simon was already at work in the cottage. So said Polly, who had given him breakfast on the porch. He hadn't wanted to come in to the breakfast nook in his work clothes, Polly explained.

So Mrs. Moffat's morning was like any other morning except for a sense of his hidden presence and a conviction of his continuing efforts. She marveled that he was no bother at all. There was no turbulence; he neither demanded nor intruded. Yet he did not cease to be thoughtful. Near noon he came quietly to report, saying that he needed more steel wool and he'd just go and get some and pick up a hamburger while he was away. He'd be back, he prophesied, by two o'clock.

Pleased with him because she wouldn't have to wonder where he was, Mrs. Moffat offered him the car, but he refused. He didn't have a driver's license at the moment, he said, and anyhow he'd rather not risk her car in the traffic. "It's pretty wild to me," he said.

So although Mrs. Moffat ate her lunch alone and took her rest as usual, her mind was full of quite unusual questions. Where in the world had he been, for pity's sake, that traffic could intimidate *him* (aged twenty-eight)? On some ship at sea? Yet sailors had shore leave, and they had it in cities, didn't they? Maybe he'd been in the Army, creeping on his belly in the mud or crawling through some jungle. But surely not all the time. More likely he'd been in a hospital, and if so—for a very long siege—and why, and where? She thought to herself crossly, *That's what you get for being selfish. You get to die of curiosity.* She wished she'd let him give her a rough outline of his troubles.

31

When she heard him returning on schedule, it came to her that she was going to be shown a shining kitchenette before the day was over. She had no doubt of it. And would it not be cruel—too cruel—not to give him the earned pleasure of cooking something out there, at least once? Mrs. Moffat was well aware of an old truth. Whatever you worked so hard to "keep," in the sense of caretaking, became in some measure your rightful possession.

She phoned the gas company and asked them to send someone to turn on the gas in her cottage. They promised to come tomorrow.

So she and Simon, who had put on his one and only suit (how could he be carrying another in that tiny bag?) took a summer supper on the porch, and in the evening, when the sun struck gold on the tops of the back and eastern hedge, but the porch lay in shadows and was deliciously cool, they sat on there together.

He had again chosen the slender bentwood rocker, and she the rocker that was padded well. His was drawn close to the screen. He seemed often to yearn outward. There was a dainty understanding between them. *She* had the privilege of rocking as much or as little as she liked, and whenever; the boy rocked only slightly and in interludes, of a sort, making himself responsible for never permitting any dizzying conflict of their rocking chair rhythms.

As Mrs. Moffat kept prattling on about one thing or another, she was no longer at all startled by her guest's red beard and head. She had accepted his appearance, as she was beginning to accept his listening presence. Oh, she knew his attention waxed and waned, and that sometimes he was listening only to sound patterns. But he was no bother. He didn't fidget.

Even so, she stopped the flood at last. "I don't know why you let me talk so much, Simon."

"I like to hear you talk, ma'am," he said lazily.

"I don't see why." If she sounded as if she were pouting, then so be it.

"You say things that I never did know," he answered soberly, "and it's wonderful to me."

Mrs. Moffat dropped the subject, too alarmingly charmed by his answer to dare pursue it.

When the phone rang, she went indoors to speak to Crystal. Would Marguerite care to come over? Joe and Flo would be glad to pick her up, and Claire had a good book from the library, so that the other four could have a game. Mrs. Moffat discovered that she did not—in the least—want to go have a game. She begged off, saying that she had company. She explained about the neighbor's child. Claire could make the fourth, couldn't she?

"Well," said Crystal, "whatever you *say*," and hung up. Miffed. Claire was a terrible bridge player, a born fourth, a last resort.

Mrs. Moffat began to tell her "company" about Crystal and Claire. They were widows of her own vintage who had taken an apartment together. On the whole they got along, but Mrs. Moffat had a hunch that sometimes it was rough going. So different. Crystal was quite a large woman. Well, the fact was, Crystal had become obese. Claire was vague. She couldn't focus long enough to worry, in Mrs. Moffat's opinion, while Crystal worried all the time and had to be eating and drinking to comfort herself.

As she laughed with affection over the foibles of her friends, she wondered if Simon could detect the affection in all that she had been saying. "This kind of catty old gossip I'll *bet* you never did know," she said. "I'm fond of them, Simon, I'm very fond. Sometimes I think I ought to ask them both to come live with me. There's space. But what if we were miserable, the three of us? It's my house. How could I put them out if once I asked them in?"

She began to wish she weren't saying this. "I talk too much," she rattled on. "I talk your head off and forget to ask how you slept in that miserable old bed, and you don't tell me."

He roused himself to speech at once. "Oh, the bed's just fine, Mrs. Moffat. I went right off, at first. But then I woke up . . . and I guess too many ghosts were fighting in my head. I couldn't go back to sleep anymore. But I could hear all kinds of little sounds, and I listened to them."

"I do that," she said in pleasure and astonishment. "I waken, and as you say, it's as if ghosts were fighting in my head. You get used to it."

"Do you?" he murmured.

"So I listen to the little sounds of all the little creatures who live here, too. When you're as old as I am, Simon, you'll have lots of time to listen to whole other worlds." She roused herself from wonder. "You ought to sleep the night through, soundly. Have you been ill, my dear?"

He didn't answer. His breath seemed caught.

(I *shouldn't have said that*, she scolded herself. "My dear" indeed!) "I think you need some solid rest and a better balanced diet than hamburgers," she said severely. "Have you written to your folks, Simon? Do they know where you are?"

"No, ma'am."

She was surprised—this thoughtful boy?

His chair was still, but not quite still. It trembled? "I don't want to talk about it, " he muttered reproachfully. "Mrs. Moffat, do you remember?" he struck out boldly. "One time, wasn't there a robbery in your house?"

"Oh, yes." She gave her chair a hard push. "Oh, yes. One summer somebody got in. I suppose *you* were small enough to think that was exciting." She felt cross with him.

"Excuse me. I can see you don't wear jewelry. Didn't you ever get the jewelry back?"

"No, no," she said. "That was a long time ago, and all forgotten. I'm not very fond of beads and things."

"I guess you had insurance?" Was he "making" talk?

"Oh, my husband," said Mrs. Moffat, "was a great believer in insurance." Now, now, she had no business being cross with him because he hadn't written to his mother. The young didn't bother to keep in touch these days. She slowed her chair. "Simon, you puzzle me," she blurted.

"I'm sorry," he said alertly. "Is it all right, ma'am, if I stay for tonight and go away in the morning?"

"Where will you go?" she said, after a moment's breathlessness.

"It doesn't matter."

"I realize," she said tartly in another moment, "that to [h]ope and whine that nothing matters is quite the thing [in s]ome circles today. But thank goodness the young are [not a]like. Some of them think things matter, and right [no]w are right to *think* so, in my opinion."

[I don't] know what to think," he murmured sullenly. [... i]t matters. Or where I should go."

Mrs. Moffat was definitely annoyed with him. "In my opinion," she said, "you should go home."

He seemed startled.

"However," she continued, "my opinion is uninformed, you will agree? So if you would prefer to stay on in the cottage for a few more days ... until the ghosts in your head fight things out to some kind of conclusion, *I* don't mind." She rocked violently. "Maybe by that time you will begin to 'know' a thing or two or at least have the human courage to imagine that you do."

His chair was motionless. Twilight was coming on. The light was tweedy now. A small, sweet breeze came by.

He said, in his soft, grainy voice, "I guess I've been wishing I could stay here a little longer. How will I know when to put myself out, though?" Was he teasing or not?

Sometimes, when he drew away and looked at her with pure curiosity, she found it stimulating and delightful—an affirmation of her existence.

This time he could be teasing. Mrs. Moffat heard a sudden playback of her staccato voice, preaching so irritably, and she sank back. Her chair rocked backward; her little feet came up from the floor. Simon scraped his own feet backward to have them under him and be ready to catch her from going all the way over. But Mrs. Moffat spoke in a voice enriched with amusement (because who needed "affirmation of her existence"? What solemn nonsense! Either she existed or she didn't. She ought to know without depending on an itinerant youth for testimony).

"When you become a bother to me, Simon," she said, "I'll mention it. Don't you worry. I have no obligation to you, remember—nor you to me, for pity's sake. So long as your staying here is pleasant for both of us, why

shouldn't you stay? I can't think of a single solitary
reason why not. Can you? I've found it pleasant as far."
she added. "So far."

He raised his head. He laughed out loud. He said,
just didn't have any idea—any *idea* . . ."

"I am quite surprised myself," she said, beaming

"Smitty didn't tell me," he crowed. Then he
if he must beware.

"Who is Smitty?" She rocked gently. She didn't care
who Smitty was. She was pleased with herself, and him,
too—with the world, the texture of time, and many things.

"This—friend of mine, ma'am."

"And what didn't Smitty tell?" she droned am

"Oh—he was just talking about his grandmoth

Mrs. Moffat started to preen herself and say s
proud about grandmotherhood, but then, reme
she did not.

"Would it be pleasant for you," he said in a
"if there were a ring of flowers around the
again?"

She rocked judiciously. "It might be. It might be."

"May I dig up a flower bed for you?" He was ea
but restrained. "Maybe your gardener—you said you
one—maybe he'd show me how to put some flowers in
don't know anything about flowers. This is just to *infor*
you, ma'am."

"Nor does Ben," she said promptly, thinking that
Simon sometimes used "ma'am" as if it were her name,
for instance, "Maggie." "He doesn't know a rose from a
violet from a bird-of-paradise. He can cut the grass and
clip and prune and spend entirely too much time hand
watering. But flowers don't mean a thing to a 'gardener' in
these parts. Not anymore. We might, I suppose, go to
some nursery and be advised."

"Could we?"

"Well, of course, we could. I seem to remember—" She
spoke of old remembered flowers, seeing them in her
mind's eye, as they had once bloomed, in a low ring
around the sundial, when the sundial had been centered
on the back lawn and not in the bay at the side. This

element of her vision she didn't mention. It didn't occur
to her to do so. How pleasant to be dredging up the
names of the blue *Agathaea?* The tiny, tiny ones? Lobel-
ia! Dianthus for pink—pinks, yes—dianthus. And
marigolds, for yellow. But you had to watch the snails to
grow marigolds. Five million, four hundred eighty-two
thousand, and *two* snails lived here. Did Simon realize?

"Couldn't we eat them?" he said, as merry as she.

"We might; we might." Mrs. Moffat was having a
wonderful time. And furthermore, she was getting used to
it. "Then, of course, there was always heartsease," she
said happily.

Upstairs at last, and in her bed and the house darkened
and all quiet, Mrs. Moffat let herself entertain a stray
thought she had had during the evening. Could it be some
form of amnesia that ailed the boy? He took no interest in
his old house, his old yard. He never mentioned his
family. What if he had been told what his name was, yet
did not really "know" it? Simon had never answered her
question about an illness. Suppose he had had what is
commonly called a mental illness? Ought she to meddle?
She said to herself, *Nonsense. How can it do him anything but good to fool around with a flower bed and eat
some decent meals at regular hours and have a place to
stay for a few nights, and a little peace? That couldn't
hurt* him *or anyone in the world! I'll do as I see to do,* she
thought, and said the Lord's Prayer, blurring the part
about "Lead us not . . ." *"Deliver us from evil."*

She woke in the deep dark, hearing the little sounds.
How could he have amnesia? What melodrama! He
remembered the sundial, didn't he? And the flowers that
used to be. He remembered Sunday school and Tommy
Moffat. A ghost stirred in her head. Strange, how he had
mentioned the time her house had been burglarized and
her "jewelry" taken. All her pretty fakes, her strings of
"pearls," and only the loss of her garnet pin to regret, and
that for "sentimental reasons." It had happened the summer that Tommy had lived here and played with Simon

Warren. Did Simon know or only half remember what
Mrs. Moffat had for years suspected? Tommy Moffat was
a thief—a thief and a fugitive from justice. Had he been a
thief already, the summer he had been eleven?

DEAR SMITTY:
   I could have dug them up last night, but I didn't know
where she keeps any tools. You said there's no hurry. Now
I've got a better idea. I'll dig them up in the daytime. She's
not going to know. It would be good if I stay here until you
figure how to cash them in.
   Listen, it takes two damn hours on the damn bus to get
where you are supposed to be, and Sunday night I took the
trouble and I couldn't find you, so I guess you get your mail.
Just don't forget your name, will ya, fella?

   The writing trailed off; the book slapped shut.

Chapter 4

BEN Guest drove his truck in early Tuesday morning and parked it where he always did—near the garage. He got out and came around to let down his tail gate and the ramp for his power mower. But then he looked across the lawn, braced, and went striding past the window behind which Mrs. Moffat was just finishing her breakfast. The sour look Ben wore reminded her that Simon had been up since dawn and was out there now, already digging around the sundial.

She hurried out and across the grass to where Simon was coiled on the ground and Ben was standing over him haranguing, gesturing, and obviously very angry.

Ben saw her and turned, growling. "He hadn't ought to make a mess like that, Mrs. Moffat. Flowers! Pah!" Ben spat. "What does he think? He's got to go pretty near to China? And I'm telling you, any of them pebbles gets jammed in my mower . . ."

"This is Simon Warren, Ben," she said firmly. "Simon, this is my gardener, Ben Guest." She became aware of Simon's work. He had removed the sod from a ring that was two feet wide, and he had dug deep. There was a rim of the dry and sandy soil around his trench. He had evidently, on hands and knees, been stirring the soil still deeper with a hand trowel. But he was coiled now, his bare toes braced, ready to spring up, his head, all covered with red lamb's wool, ready to butt.

"Whyncha wait till *I* come?" Ben was snarling. "Who's going to edge that thing, I'm asking you, and who's going to comb them stones out of my mower's way?"

Simon spoke before she could. "I am," he said.

"Damn right," said Ben. "*I'm* not."

Mrs. Moffat, to her surprise, kept still.

Ben was reacting to the beard. Simon was reacting to hostility. He came up with a slow rippling of muscles; he rose with hard control and a readiness that had dark warning in it.

Ben felt it, too. He said, "Listen, Miz Moffat, if you gave him permission, that's one thing—"

"I told you that she had," said Simon indifferently, as if it were too late now. Ben must be punished.

"Well, *listen*," Ben said, stepping backward. "I hadda *check*. Don't look to me you know what you're doing," he flared. "And if Miz Moffat don't want me to do her yard work no more, let her say so."

Mrs. Moffat (who was inwardly tickled to pieces) said serenely, "I think you had better go and do the work you are hired to do, if you please, Ben. Mr. Warren and I have a little project here, and we are going to have some fun with it. However, when we have finished, I would suggest that *you* rake the pebbles out of the lawn, since you know best about your mower, don't you?"

Ben mumbled. He spat, and just missed, the tip of her cane and her neat black shoe. Simon's eyes flashed. The words on the tip of his tongue were words Mrs. Moffat knew primarily from reading novels. He did not speak them. Ben swallowed the same kinds of words and walked away.

Mrs. Moffat tried not to smile, but she knew her eyes were laughing. The boy had turned to watch her face intently. He was serious. He didn't answer her mischief with even the suggestion of a wink. He knew she was *delighted,* and he was wondering why.

Well, she couldn't tell him why. How could she say she was glad to discover that he had some force in him, that he was not boneless? Something in their relationship shifted over to another position. She said, trying out her own kind of force, showing it forth gently but deliberately, "Simon, I would like it very much if you could be ready by ten thirty to go with me on some errands. You can help me with my packages; we can stop in at the nursery.

And I also think that you must have some work shoes. Something very cheap will do, don't you think so?"

But now he sent some mischief back, "Yes, ma'am," he said, with the shadow of an extra syllable. Ma'ama.

"That's a very fine trench, my friend," she said, grinning at him. "It'll make a good deep foundation."

"For heartsease," he said, hiding in the beard.

She bought him some sneakers and another pair of work pants, and then knowing that for some reason she could do today what she could not have done yesterday, she said she was beginning to tire of seeing him in a suit coat every evening, and since sports shirts were perfectly acceptable, especially on informal occasions in the summer, she intended him to have at least two of them. She chose two cool cotton sports shirts, taking care that they were not expensive. Simon took out some money and paid for the sports shirts. Mrs. Moffat deferred to this, offering no objection. Side by side they walked out to the car, Mrs. Moffat demurely pleased with them both.

Crystal Adams said to Flo Keating, on the phone, "We can't help being *concerned* about Marguerite Moffat. When Claire and I ran into them in the market, we couldn't believe it! There was Marguerite running around with this *young* man, this very young man, at her heels like a puppy dog. And Flo, dear, he is an absolutely *weird*-looking character ... A beard! Oh, *all* over his face, and *red!* Oh, yes, and all in little curls, like something off a frieze. I can't tell you how startled we were. They seemed—chummy."

"Do you mean he is staying on with her?"

"Well, that was certainly what she implied! And after all, even if he used to live next door when he was a little boy, it's all very well to be kind, but we wonder whether Marguerite is being wise."

"Do you think Joe ought to take a look at him?"

"Oh, I was hoping you might say just that. Yes, I do, Flo. After all, a *man* ..."

"I'll see if he wants to drop in on Marguerite and let

you know. I'm dying to see him *myself*. I never heard of such a thing. You say 'chummy'?"

"Definitely," said Crystal in mournful tones.

At four o'clock, Simon, wearing the blue sports shirt, was sitting in what had become "his" rocker, poring over the garden book they had purchased at the nursery. Mrs. Moffat watched him contentedly.

When Joe and Flo rang the front doorbell and Polly let them in, Mrs. Moffat heard their voices and went into the house to greet them.

She knew at once exactly why they had come, so she hung back teasingly, enjoining them to sit down indoors. Flo had a way of letting her pupils fly upward and to the right when she was socially nervous, which was often. But Joe, who had spent his married life scoffing at social nerves, came out with it bluntly. They'd heard she had some young fellow staying here. Was he still here, and if so, where was he?

Simon was so absorbed in what he was reading that he did not at first take any notice when they came parading to the porch.

"Here are some friends of mine, come to call," said Mrs. Moffat.

He leaped to his feet. "I'm sorry. Oh, I'm *s-sorry*."

"Flo, this is Simon Warren—Mrs. Keating. And Mr. Keating, Simon."

Joe held out his right hand automatically and said, "Your folks used to live next door, eh? How long ago was that?"

But the skin of Simon's face, what could be seen of it, had flushed. He seemed hideously embarrassed. "Very nice," he said, backing away. "Very nice to meet you, Mrs. Keating, ma'am—sir. Would you please excuse me? Mrs. Moffat, may I please go out to my room?" He was already backed against the screen door. He seemed shy as a deer.

No, he isn't, she thought grimly. *He wants out, and he's getting out, and he means to have his way.*

She said graciously, "Why, of course, Simon—but do come back and chat if you can?"

"Yes, ma'am," he said, with a look that gave *her* the score. He wouldn't. He slipped outside. He ran on the grass and vanished onto the path that led to the cottage.

Somewhat troubled by a glimpse, a flash, a picture in her mind, Mrs. Moffat begged her old friends to sit down.

After a few minutes of Joe's exhaustive questioning Mrs. Moffat began to be glad that Simon had run away. She answered as best she could. "Just out of the service," she told them, a statement which would have to do. Herself, she had never asked how long "a little while" had been. On his way home, of course. At least, she assumed so. She watered down that lie. But he had cleaned out the old cottage for her, and so beautifully. Naturally she had asked him to stay on a bit out there. He was such a nice boy, and polite and helpful. She would quite enjoy entertaining him for a brief but indefinite period. Flo said, "He's awfully shy isn't he, Marguerite?"

"He seems so," Mrs. Moffat equivocated.

Joe had to know exactly when the Warrens had moved away and where they had gone and how old Simon had been at the time and how many years he had been in the service and which branch.

Mrs. Moffat became vague and offered tea or something stronger.

Joe took beer and went right on asking questions. "Why does a kid like that want to wear all those whiskers? Crazy," said Joe.

"Oh, now, Joe," said Flo, "they all do."

"What I say—you never know what's hiding under a mass of whiskers," Joe said. His clean-shaven cheeks sagged in dewlaps. No matter what Joe felt he always looked as sad as a bloodhound. "From what I hear today, I wouldn't give one of those beards the house room."

"But he's not staying in the house," said Flo, betraying her thoughts. "He isn't in the house at night."

Mrs. Moffat chided her friends for being "silly" and imperiously turned the talk to something else. Flo's eyes were full of fear that they had offended, and she, too, kept the barricade. Joe subsided.

Simon had vanished; he did reappear.

When Joe and Flo had given up and gone away, their hostess sat by herself on the porch, swaying gently. She *wasn't* offended. She had been a little startled. She ought not resent their concern, dear old Flo and Joe. Tender-and-gruff. Ah, well . . .

Polly came for the glass and the teacups.

Shall I ask Polly? thought Mrs. Moffat. *She might remember.* But she did not ask Polly, because Polly might indeed remember, and the truth was Mrs. Moffat did not wish to risk being confirmed in a freakish suspicion that she was ashamed to mention. No, no, she must be wrong. She was probably thinking of some other neighbor's boy . . . whichever one she had suddenly seen in her memory's eye, racing after Tommy Moffat across her yard, Tommy's blue-black head in the lead and a towhead bouncing after.

DEAR SMITTY:

It really was funny. You'd have got a laugh out of it. These characters came to call, see, and I forgot. I absolutely forgot I've got all this hair on my face—and I'm thinner, and all that. First thing that hit me—They'll recognize! They'll know me from the pictures in the paper! So I ran like hell. Then I had to laugh.

Listen, I've got some sad news. I guess your old buddy's been by the sundial himself, unless a couple of scared little kids didn't remember straight. Believe me, the stuff isn't where you told me. And I should know, because (like her gardener said) I pretty near got through to China. (Is *that* a laugh?)

Listen, it seems to me now, you were probably better off . . .

The pencil stopped, returned, and made thick and furious strokes over the last sentence. The notebook closed.

Chapter 5

TIME was a lake. It must have its feeding springs and its outlets, since it was not stagnant, yet there was no turbulence. The golden days went dimpling and rippling by.

Mrs. Moffat's guest, or servant, or protégé, was in and out of the grounds. Whenever he left, he told her when to expect him back again. He did not always tell her where he was going, especially in the evenings.

She wondered about girls. Mrs. Moffat was not so old or so forgetful that she didn't imagine he might need a girl. Well, then—that being his business and surely not hers—perhaps he found a girl from time to time. Mrs. Moffat wasn't so innocent or so ignorant that she could suppose there were no girls to be found. He was twenty-eight and had been to the wars. No celibate he. She was only moderately curious, having never herself been a young man in a strange city in need of a girl, about *how* they were to be found. A boy would know. She was, in fact, much comforted by these thoughts, because if he had settled in and never, never chosen to leave her place or her company, then, indeed, she would have been forced to ask herself what about girls? She was glad that he did not imprison himself here. If she wanted to be cold-blooded about it, this was not only because she needn't worry about girls too much, but because she could also conclude that Simon felt no need to be in hiding (under a beard) and hidden all around. No, no, Mrs. Moffat cast off the negatives.

She would never ask Simon why he had run from the Keatings. Why ask, when she knew? Joe was transparent enough to be read in an instant. Catechism was his style. Mrs. Moffat was foxier than that.

She was glad Simon did not confine himself. She was

ashamed of the thought that this meant he felt no need to hide. No, she was glad for his sake, if to try out the—well, call it traffic—from home base was a learning process. Perhaps he was beginning to "recognize" things. For herself, the lonely evenings were excellent for balance. She enjoyed them, too.

When he was what she thought of as "at home," he seemed to have drawn up limits for himself. The cottage he accepted as his place. He had told Polly not to bother. He felt perfectly free on the grounds. But he had never ventured very far into her house. He would come willingly to the porch, although he always kept to the outer portion of it.

The first time she invited him to watch television with her Simon declined. He would rather read, he said. So she gave him books; she gave him classics. *They* wouldn't hurt him, and besides, classics were what she owned in abundance. But the books he craved as if he were starving were garden books. He didn't say so, but Mrs. Moffat could perfectly well see, and she searched out all that her husband had ever acquired, and she picked up nursery catalogues around town, which he also studied with a passion, as he studied all that grew. He inspected the ring around the sundial every hour on the hour, or so it seemed, and was sent into a trance when a plant had taken hold. She would see him full length on the grass, fascinated by a single seedling.

They toured the territory every day, and every day she told him less, and he told her more. He was a fountain of botanical names.

Once when she found a California poppy that had gone to seed and showed him the tiny exquisite pagoda and the shining black dots within, he became so still, in contemplation, that she held her breath. He was gone into the texture of time. He had sunk into its vertical dimensions? Oh, my! She breathed again, wondering what she had *meant* by such thoughts, but not pressing for the answers.

On Sunday morning Mrs. Moffat went to church alone. Simon confessed that he really didn't want to go. He didn't understand what was said and done there; he guessed he never had. Could he please be excused?

She did not coax him. He was looking well. She could even imagine that he had gained some solid flesh. His head was brilliant in the sun. She thought, *Let him worship in the garden. What will God care?*

That day (in meditation) Mrs. Moffat was able to identify what it was about him that so appealed to her. He was considerate and clean and industrious. All these traits had been praiseworthy in her prime. But what really fascinated and held her was her growing conviction of the boy's capacity for being happy. (His only just lightly crusted over, his rising, his ready-to-burst talent and need.) So long as she kept away from any mention of his family, his worldly fortunes, his recent past, or anything to do with *reasons* for confusion or sadness, he was on the very brink of a childlike and primitive joy, and sometimes when he succumbed, Mrs. Moffat both rejoiced and trembled. To see a young person—or anybody else for that matter—just plain and perfectly *happy* was the most pleasant and exhilarating sight in the world. And very rare. She could not resist the temptation to throw him in the way of such a mood . . . and she was beginning to be quite clever about it, too.

But at the same time, she felt guilty because it was poor preparation for life outside her private paradise. For traffic? Almost nobody over the age of ten admitted to feeling this kind of happiness anymore; in an adult it was definitely suspect. Oh, this kind of happiness had been out of fashion even in Mrs. Moffat's youth. It was not a fashion. It was an older phenomenon than fashion. Simply to *see* it was enchanting.

Ah, well, I'm a selfish old woman, she said to herself, *and I'll do as I please, while I may.*

She couldn't kid herself that golden days went on forever.

One evening when Simon, who had spent the whole day in the open area of her yard, was drowsing in his chair, Mrs. Moffat got on to the subject of Cynthia. "My son, Thomas," she was saying, "as I think I've told you, was never physically as strong as people ought to be. I must have overprotected him, as they say today. If so, then so be it. You never did meet my son's wife, Cynthia. You wouldn't have paid her any mind if you had. I did not want them to marry. That was an instinct, I think now. I couldn't argue. I was afraid to *seem* jealous." Mrs. Moffat was nodding like a puppet with its head on a string. She stiffened her neck and said, "I *was* jealous, all right. Among other things. I sometimes wonder, looking back, whether I protected him enough. Cynthia was a year or two older than he, a decisive, enterprising woman, very strong—or so she seemed. And what 'seeming' notions!" Mrs. Moffat snorted. "Cynthia would stride into a room, Simon. She had big bones and strong feet, and oh, she put them *down*. She would lay out, in a loud voice, some noble plan; she'd have every step organized, driving very logically and intelligently toward some goal. *That* was going to be *it*. But the next week, you see, or sometimes the very next day, she would produce an equally well-ordered but entirely different ambition. She was the least decisive, or perhaps I should say the least persistent, person I've ever known. Poor child, Tommy, to be hers."

There. She had broken her own rule. Simon was listening peacefully. If he had noticed, he gave no sign.

"Now I don't necessarily subscribe," she said, "to the doctrine that children are molded like little pieces of putty by the ignorant or misguided fingers of adults, whence stemmeth all their problems, so that the buck never stops until Adam and Eve, if then. I do believe *that* theory needs some modification." (What a pleasure it was to speak her mind and use whatever words she cared to use. This was a thing that had been creeping and growing. Simon accepted, without fidgeting, and seemed to absorb, in some curious way of his own, everything she said in whatever language. And gradually she was trusting him to do so.)

"But I think now," she continued, "that a child who is denied his chance to put forth tendrils of his own, and take some hold, is a poor unlucky little child.

"Cynthia is dead now," Mrs. Moffat rushed on, "and we used to say of the dead nothing but good. But times have changed. After Thomas died, Cynthia immediately resolved to take a job and put her little one—he was only three—into a nursery school. Well, that lasted six months perhaps. Then she decided to put him with a foster family. She had a hundred reasons why, all quite sound. And that lasted . . . oh, a little while. All of a sudden it was her duty to stay at home and raise him herself, but that turned out not to be wise. I forget why. So to another foster family. *Another* would be better, of course. Far fields, Simon, always far fields. If Cynthia was in the East, she longed for the benefits of the glorious West. In the West, the advantages of the East rose up. The one year—the one summer—when at last she let us have him . . . it had been promised. We had understood that we could keep him and, I suppose, mold him until he was grown."

Simon was silent.

"She came and took him away in September," said Mrs. Moffat sadly. "You wouldn't have understood what was happening. I was too old a woman . . . too old even then. My husband had his business in the daytime. I simply wasn't spry enough. So we let him go. Oh, he was a handful that summer," she said, painfully bright, "and so were you, as I remember."

He didn't respond. His eyes kept wide open, regarding her with that opaque look he so often had. His owl look, she called it to herself. There were a few more words, bitter in her mouth, and she let them out. "His mother taught him nothing. She picked him up; she threw him down; she gave him to this one or that one; she snatched him back. He had no chance. The best I can do, to forgive her, is tell myself she had no idea what she was doing—and I can almost believe it, because neither did I, at that time." Her head bent in old sorrow.

Simon stirred.

"Never mind," she said, and dropped him all the way out of her attention. This boy was not her grandson who had been lost so long ago. He was only a passing stranger, a temporary playmate for the old lady, an entertainment.

Simon said, in a moment, "Like a seedling, do you mean, Mrs. Moffat, that you transplant too often?"

"I suppose," she said listlessly. The analogy wasn't perfect. Let it go.

"I can see," he said solemnly, "that you ought to persist, on the way to a goal."

Mrs. Moffat didn't respond. If he was demonstrating that he had been listening all along, trying to please her, he wasn't succeeding.

He thinks I was preaching, she mused. *Perhaps I was.*

"If I could have a goal, Mrs. Moffat, I think I know now what it would be."

"You do?" she sighed indifferently.

"Working with plants!" He was breathless, as if he were revealing a great secret.

"Why not, then?" said Mrs. Moffat carelessly. She was very tired. She wished she were in her bed and all voices still.

"*They* aren't trying to mold anybody," he said with something of a spark, as if she had asked him why. "*Plants* don't tell you this is right and that is wrong and tell you something else tomorrow. Plants aren't confusing. I don't think they *are* confused. That's wonderful to me."

"Oh, you're never going to fool a rose," she said, rousing herself to some courteous animation. "It needs what it needs—that's all *it* knows. So if it's lucky, it buds and blooms and fades and makes some seed—or a wild rose may—and what seeds are lucky will do the same." She would go up to bed as soon as she felt a little less depressed and a little more competent to get there.

"You believe in *luck?*" he said alertly.

"Of course I do," she said wearily. "Too many things go on that we haven't any other name for." Mrs. Moffat was exhausted. She had talked too much. She didn't want to talk for days and days.

"Luck," he was murmuring. "It must be good luck just to be here."

Oh, child, she thought, *teach your grandmother.* Was he dreaming of becoming her gardener, another old Mr.

McGregor, aged twenty-eight? What about girls? What about marriage? Blooming and seeding? She said nothing.

"I could learn to be a gardener," Simon was saying. "I could persist. If I wasn't so afraid that everything's too late for me. There are too many things I can't change now." He bit his knuckle. "Do you think I could be a gardener?"

"How should I know," she said, "whether you can or not, or what your luck will be? For your information, Simon, old ladies are much tempted to play the wise old women. But the truth is, old women *are* old, and their maxims are old stuff. Who knows if they hold? Don't sit at my feet, you silly man, in a world-and-time that's through with me."

"Don't, " he said, startled and as if she were giving him pain.

She had given herself pain. "Things change and people die. I don't suppose you can imagine how little I will mind."

"What if I can?" He breathed. "Because to me sometimes it seems like the peaceful answer."

Mrs. Moffat's conscience woke up screaming. *No, no, no, no,* thought Mrs. Moffat. *This is wrong—worry and strife—this isn't any fun at all.*

"By the way, Simon," she said briskly, brushing all moping and whining aside, "I've had a letter from my granddaughter. She'll be here on the tenth."

He turned away sadly.

"Simon?"

Sometimes he wouldn't rouse, even when she called his name.

"I can tell you," said Mrs. Moffat, "that Zan doesn't give a hoot about plants and gardens. That I'm sure of. She's a city girl, Zan is. She has a friend who takes her out, you know. She doesn't ..." Mrs. Moffat was about to say, "Hang around all the time and listen to *my* philosophy," but she shut her mouth.

"How many days before she comes?" he asked drearily.

Mrs. Moffat pretended not to have heard. If she had

meant that he must leave, she wouldn't have given the message obliquely. He ought to know *that* by now. But she couldn't scold him. She was sorry that she had let her own spirits spiral downward during this evening. She was sorry to see him enfolded by that mysterious numbness.

"I have a surprise for you," she said, rallying all her forces. "Something I don't believe you've noticed in all your snoopings and prowlings."

"Yes, ma'am?" He was polite.

"There's a big concrete bin sunk in the ground out behind the garage. Mr. McGregor used to use it for his compost heap.

She watched him waken. (Oh, yes, he had read all about compost!)

"But how long has it been there?" he gasped. "Oh, Mrs. Moffat, if it's full and it's been working all these years——"

"It may be very ripe and rich," she said, "or all the good leached out of it, for all I know. You'd better go see in the morning."

"*As good as magic,* she thought, watching him yearn toward the dark garden. Her own heart was lightening. "You look as if you just found the map to the buried treasure," she teased him.

But when she was abed, she thought, *What did I hear? What did he say? What have I done? Tossed him a bit of bait? The illusion of a goal? The news of a smelly old compost heap because I knew he would rejoice? But sliding myself out from under whatever dark old sorrows he may have been ready to let me help him carry?*

The truth is, I do not want a piece of his past sorrow. I would much prefer to see him happy every day. If he has a past to hash over and reinterpret, let his ghosts fight it out in his head. I may be a wicked old woman, to keep tricking him into patches of job for the sake of the pleasure it gives me. But if so, so be it. Let him take his risks, she thought grumpily, and turned her cheek to the pillow.

A fire escape ran by the open window. The air that rose up from the dirty downtown Los Angeles street at one o'clock in the morning was somewhat less foul than the air in this room.

"I can stay there," said the red-bearded boy who was sitting on the windowsill, "for a while."

"There has got to be a way," said the man who was lying on the bed. "I'm thinking. While I'm doing that, you stay there."

"I don't like this crummy room, when I'm in a better place. You know that."

"Don't worry. I've met a girl who's got a better place. I come here for the mail. By the way, thanks for your name."

"That's okay."

The only light came from a bare bulb in the ceiling. The man on the bed had the crook of his elbow over his eyes to shield them from the glare.

"Say, Smitty, speaking of girls, your cousin (I guess she must be) is showing up on the tenth."

"What cousin is this?" said the man in a moment.

"Zan, they call her."

A police car screamed by below, and the red-bearded boy looked out the window to watch its progress. The man on the bed had become rigid.

"Alexandra is her real name, I think," said the boy in the window. "Alexandra Terry. She runs some business in New York. Mrs. Moffat says she comes out every summer."

"I'll think about it," said the man on the bed thickly.

"You feeling okay?"

"All but my leg," the man said in a vicious snarl.

The red-bearded boy stood up.

"It aches like hell, and it always will," said Smitty, "but you're the one who's blaming you. I never said so." He took his arm away from his unshaved face. His eyes were odd. One seemed almost sealed shut by a melting and rehardening of the flesh and bone of his brow.

"You're sure you've got the medicine for far enough

ahead?" said his visitor. "You're keeping the money for it?"

"Sure. Sure. The tenth, you say?" The man rolled and put his feet to the floor. "Hang in there, baby. Be nice to Zan, but not too nice."

When his voice stopped, the red-bearded boy kept right on listening intently, so the man said, "You stick to the old lady. Zan's not for you. One of these days, when I figure how to put the proposition, somebody's going to pay the two of us for staying out of their lives. That's all we've got to sell, old buddy. Yah, Zan's a girl. So what? I know where there's girls in Mexico. Listen, I'd tell you more, but I'm interested to see what they do. I want to think about it."

"That's okay," said the boy.

Chapter 6

AT 3 P.M. Los Angeles time Zan walked off the jet, was met, kissed and complimented, and carried off into the maze of the city in Nicky's car. It was agreed that she must be taken at once to Mrs. Moffat's house, where she would stay close for a day or two. Zan did believe that by Wednesday her grandmother might be just as glad to be rid of her for dinner and the evening. "She's used to being quiet," Zan explained. "She will have had it on chit-chat, so you may appear then."

"Wouldn't it be sensible," said Nicky plaintively, "for you to give a me a carbon copy of your fortnit's shedyool? My secretary could compare it with mine, and we'd know where we were, wouldn't we?"

"For God's sake, Nicky!" said Zan mildly.

"You career females tend to assume you can have it both ways. Say please?" He was grinning.

"Oh, please forgive me," she said sweetly, "for assuming Wednesday."

"No need to be sickening. Wise, however, to set a tone. We shall assume Wednesday."

"Very well," she said briskly.

But Zan grinned to herself. She had looked at Nicky Pomerance with different eyes this time, and was even now taking note of all she could see of this place, this city, with the same difference. How would everything seem if she were not a visitor? What if she lived here?

And ah so! . . . Nicky had looked at her with a difference, too. Why else would it have crossed his mind to "set a tone"?

When they arrived, Nicky begged off any part of the meeting and greeting. He pleaded his working day and his abhorrence of sherry, carried her bags as far as the front door, kissed her with definite relish, and ducked away.

"Oh, Miss Zan!" cried Polly. "You're here!"

So Alexandra Terry Moffat drew in her breath and entered the old house that would someday belong to her. Not that *she* could ever live here. It was too—well—buried and muffled over. Zan thought in terms of some high place—glass and vistas. The dim square hall with the white balustered staircase was just the same. Zan put her bags at the bottom of the stairs, forbade Polly to touch them, kissed that old cheek lightly, and went on to the sitting room to find the old lady of the house, who was just the same.

Zan embraced Mrs. Moffat with tender gusto, exclaimed over the room, which was just the same and always both amused and subtly annoyed her. Then she flew up the stairs, bags and all, and dumped them in the bedroom at the back, which was always hers. She fished out shorts and shirt and returned, bare-legged, to sit down, take the inevitable sherry (the proper prescription for the reviving of travelers) and began to ask the same fond questions.

"Have you been well, Gran? You're looking awfully darned healthy, seems to me."

The old lady, of course, had not gotten any younger. But the year just past did not seem to have touched her very much. Her color was good; her eyes were bright. Her white hair was twisted up into the same comical little knot; Zan had to admit the style became the tilt of the old lady's nose.

The only name she had for Mrs. Moffat was Gran. Alexandra Terry could have called herself a Mrs. Moffat, but she had taken to her maiden name when she had re-entered college. And had kept it. It suited her. It was, for one thing, her own name.

"Tell me what you've been up to," she said. "How are Crystal and Claire? And the Keatings?" Zan felt intimations of mortality to be mentioning these old, old people. One day she'd ask and one of them would have died.

Mrs. Moffat said that she hadn't seen Crystal and

Claire for some time now. She hadn't seen a great deal of Joe and Flo either. Zan caught a flicker of guilt. The fact was, Mrs. Moffat confessed, she had been preoccupied with the garden.

"The garden!"

The fact was, Mrs. Moffat went on gaily, she had a young man staying in the old cottage, and he and she had been quite busy working out some improvements in the landscaping.

"Hi ho, what's all this?" Zan teased. "You've got a young man on the premises? Who is he?"

Zan felt her face become more and more bland as she listened to Mrs. Moffat's tale of a young man who had lived next door when a child, who had come by to revisit old familiar places, who was at a bit of a loose end personally, who was taking such an interest.

"How long has he been here?"

"Oh, a few weeks. Not long. Now Zan, I do hope you are not going to try to boss *him* around."

"Why, Gran! Whatever *are* you saying!"

But Zan was thinking to herself: *A few weeks, but not long? What kind of statement is that?*

"You know very well," said Mrs. Moffat severely, "that it's your tendency to boss people around. I don't mind. I'm old and tougher than you are. But I wish . . . Just let him be, will you please, dear? Don't go asking him a great long list of questions."

"But why not?" said Zan lightly. "And haven't you?"

"I simply think," said Mrs. Moffat, "that the boy has been through some very bitter experience, and he is better off not thinking about it. He has to start again. If he finds it a steadying thing to be here and be quiet—"

Zan said indulgently, "You're fond of him?"

"Yes—yes—he's a nice boy."

"Where is he now?" (*Where have you got him stashed away, sly puss, while you warn me what I mustn't do,* Zan thought, *to this nice boy?*)

"He's on the grounds somewhere," said Mrs. Moffat. "Will you go find him and ask him to come take a cup of tea?"

"Of course I will." Zan went across the back porch, moving silently on her lithe legs, and out into the deep shade of the big acacia. If this "nice boy" had been scrounging off the old lady on the strength of some sob story, Zan would soon see about that.

She caught sight of a figure, crouched with a bent back toward her, deep into her grandmother's plot, all the way to the end. So Zan ambled on the grass over patterns of sun and shade, sniffing the unfamiliar perfume in this air, peering on all sides, and thinking of many things. She must make some phone calls, set up appointments, go talk to people, see how available was her grandmother's car, rent one perhaps, and (one day) find out how the zoning laws read for this street and what might be done with so large, so deep a piece of ground, so hidden, and somehow so out of it, so drowsy and drenched in green and golden silence.

She had come within a few yards of the figure when her feet stabbed the ground and stopped her. Wait! What was this!

He had turned and was in profile to her. He was kneeling now; his hands were busy in some bare soil at the base of the hedge. His head was bent. He was absorbed. It was as if Zan were staring at a painting, a complex of greens for background, and the soft faded blue of the trousers, the flesh tones of the naked torso, flushed a pinky brown, and then that bright copper—no—bronze, but bronze that twinkled with gold . . . the *blaze* of that head and face . . . all light caught in those tight and shining coils. It would have been a picture conceived by some Renaissance fellow who, having the church for his patron, must paint a young saint in a monastery garden. But his model . . . his model he had snatched off some ancient street corner, one of the boys—who, nevertheless, in pagan innocence could worship earth.

Breath cannot be held forever. He heard her gasp and turned his face. He rose to his feet easily. Zan, coolly recovered, went close enough to hold out her right hand in the forthright manner of a career girl. "Hi. You must be Simon Warren. I'm Alexandra Terry."

"Hi," he said. "Excuse me, Miss Terry." He turned up his palms, all encrusted with dark soil. "Mrs. Moffat said you were coming today."

His voice was soft. What he said was innocuous.

"She's sent me to ask you to come have some tea," said Zan, sticking to one-syllable words herself. "I think she wants us to meet."

"Yes, I'm sure." He smiled. "I'll have to get cleaned up." He moved and she turned to walk beside him.

"Were you making mud pies or what?" she asked saucily.

"Your grandmother *said* you were a city girl."

"Oh, she did? Well, that's just because she's scared I'm going to mess up your glorious plans. Don't worry, I won't."

"I don't know how glorious they are. We're just doing it for fun. I'm only learning."

All this was amiable.

But now their steps were marching and matching exactly. This was in some way uncontrollable. Compulsive. Hypnotic. They were moving in exactly the same rhythm. It was embarrassing. He must have felt it, too. He broke his stride, but in the very same second of time so did she, and it seemed they had done a little dance step together as perfectly as if they had practiced it for days. Zan could feel her face flushing. But this was ridiculous! So she stopped in her tracks. He took one step more. He turned.

"We should go on the stage," she said flippantly.

He was only an inch or two taller than she. Their eyes met easily. He seemed amused. But now a current, a wave of such animal warmth, began to flow that Zan braced herself against tottering. He must have felt it, too. His eyes turned wary and sad. He took two quick steps backward. And now she knew her open face was saying, *What's the matter? I don't necessarily mind.*

He said, "Will you please say I'll be right there, Miss Alexandra?" As if he were what? A servant?

"Why, sure enough," said Zan with a shrug. She struck off on a tangent, alone, in a strong, swinging gait.

She was distressed, not to say alarmed. Perhaps she was

angry. Oh, he had it (whatever "it" was). Oh, he had it, all right. Now did it (whatever it was) operate on a female aged seventy-four? Zan wasn't sure. But the whole *idea* was making her definitely furious now.

Mrs. Moffat was on the porch, ensconced in the padded rocking chair. Zan let the door bang as much as it would behind her and let out her breath in a gusty half whistle. "Whew! What in the world kind of exotic bird have you got out there, Gran?"

"You mean his beard?" said Mrs. Moffat flatly. "I should have warned you. I forgot."

"Forgot!" Zan gasped. She plopped herself down in the bentwood rocker. "Gran, are you trotting around this town with him and his beard in tow? I'll *betcha* Crystal and Claire are scandalized. Have they met him?"

"Yes, yes, in the market one day."

"He takes you to market?"

"I do the driving," said Mrs. Moffat.

Zan made her chair fall forward and doubled over, forearms on her thighs. "You're not telling me that he can't drive a car?" (Could a saint? Could a satyr?)

"He prefers not to," said Mrs. Moffat.

Zan lifted both arms and rocked backward. "For God's sake, Gran! Why!"

"I don't inquire——" said the old lady. "Zan, dear, do you mind sitting somewhere else?"

"What?"

"That's Simon's chair."

Zan got up; her heart was sinking (or else it was the pit of her stomach). She thought, *Oh, God, has she been this lonely?* She sat down on the settee and ran her right hand over her forehead, pushing hard at the bone. "I can't help wondering what he's doing here," she said. "Don't ask me to help that."

"He is being my guest," the old lady said emphatically, "and I may say Simon is very much the gentleman, in *spite* of his appearance. I shouldn't have supposed that, of all things in the world, a beard would have scandalized *you*."

"Just say I didn't expect one in *your* backyard," said Zan.

The little old lady in the big old chair seemed to Zan suddenly very fragile, very precious. All the weight fell on the California side of the balance. "Speaking of guests," Zan said, "I might as well break some news. Just as soon as I can get things whacked around, I'm moving out here. To live, Gran. So you'll have to put up with me in and out all year round. How's that?"

"Well!" said her grandmother, bringing her little hands together as if to applaud. "But what about your business?"

Zan was still talking about her business when Simon came to the screen door, opened it gently, and entered. He was immaculate, in a pale-yellow sports shirt, and as startling as before.

Zan saw the old lady's face soften. "Alexandra, this is Simon Warren."

"We've met," drawled Zan.

"We introduced ourselves, ma'am," Simon nodded cheerfully and sat down in the bentwood rocker.

"Polly is going to give us a company tea," said Mrs. Moffat happily. "Simon isn't joining us for dinner tonight," she told Zan. "Sometimes, you know, he is absolutely compelled to go off in quest of one of his beloved hamburgers. That used to be his single dish, gourmet that he was."

"I've tried to convince her," said Simon to Zan, "that hamburgers are actually food, but she still thinks they are treats for children, like ice-cream cones."

Mrs. Moffat was rocking in deep and satisfying arcs. "Nonsense. The truth is," she said to Zan, "he was addicted. He still suffers withdrawal symptoms."

They were not talking to Zan. No. They were so close that they had a code going; they had old jokes not funny to an outsider.

It was not long before Zan, who was sensitive to rhythms, perceived the young man's art by which he never set his chair into a contrary or disruptive motion.

He has got to be phony, Zan thought furiously. *What goes on here!*

What seemed to be going on was a tea party, with real tea. Polly came with silver pot and plate of dainty cakes, to fuss over the "company." This was Zan, who could do nothing but go along with the ceremonies, taking care that she did not *seem* either shocked or disapproving. What was there to disapprove of? A cup of tea, a cake or two? A summer porch, on a soft afternoon, everything genteel, everything kind, a party out-of-time, away from trade. No snaps, no tensions, no witty barbs, no sparks. Any electricity such as may flow between male and female was turned off as if it had never been.

Yet when Simon made polite farewells and went away, it became plain that there must have been a potential—a possibility of arcing—because the atmosphere went flat and stale so suddenly.

Later on Zan and Mrs. Moffat dined in the dining room. "My goodness," said Polly innocently, as she bustled in with the platter, "we haven't used this room all summer."

"If this formality is in my honor, forget it," said Zan, who had put on a dress. "It can't be too chilly to eat on the porch."

"Tomorrow," promised Mrs. Moffat. "Simon will be eating with us tomorrow night."

"He always likes for me to set the table on the porch," said Polly happily.

Are they both enchanted? Or what? Zan wondered.

When the meal was over, she insisted on carrying the last of the dishes out to Polly and tackled that old lady fiercely.

"How long has Simon been living out there, Polly?"

"Oh, let me see. It's more than a month, I know that. Oh, five or maybe it's six weeks, Miss Zan, dear."

"Any rumors about when he's moving out?"

"No, no," said Polly. "Oh, there's a lot to be done, and he's a worker, Miss Zan."

"He is, eh?"

"Oh, yes, and no bother at all. Why, he takes all the care of the cottage and his own laundry. He won't let me touch it. And he's so good to *her!* Why, they talk and they talk. She hasn't had time at all to think of her aches and pains."

"How old is he?" Zan demanded in a minute.

"Why, he's just exactly young Tommy's age," said Polly, her eyes sliding. "They used to play—two little boys together. Real chums. Good friends."

Oh, no, thought Zan to herself in shock. *Oh, no. Oh, no!*

Bedtime was early by the clock; normal enough on New York time. But once in negligee, Zan, with hairbrush whacking her skull, crossed the upstairs hall and tapped on Mrs. Moffat's door. The old lady was abed, propped up with a book, snug and immaculate in rosy light.

"Gran, I have to tell you something else. I hope it won't upset you. I went home, because we were married there, to get a divorce. But instead, I've had Tommy declared legally dead. You see, it could be not only that I'll want to marry again, but other legal things."

"I know, dear," said her grandmother, who had looked stricken for a moment but rallied. "You should marry, I think. You should."

"And I had to get it clear, you see . . ."

"Yes, of course."

"Gran, this Simon of yours is supposed to have known Tommy?"

"Yes. When they were children."

"Do you think he may have seen Tommy—since?"

"I don't know," said Mrs. Moffat. "We have a kind of understanding."

"So I see," said Zan softly.

"I don't pry into his sorrows, whatever they may be. Sometimes I think he may have blanked them out, Zan. The other side of the bargain is—he hasn't mentioned Tommy since the first day. I asked him not to."

"Ah, so?" said Zan thoughtfully. "That's why he didn't mention Tommy to me."

The old lady pulled down her chin and pressed her head deeper into the pillow behind it. "I don't suppose he realizes that you were Tommy's wife," she said. "No one has said so. He wouldn't ask—or even wonder in what way you are my granddaughter. Why should he?"

Zan thought, *Well, then, if he ever has run into Tommy grown up, Tommy didn't bother to say, "Oh, by the way, I have a wife, and for all I know, a child."*

The old lady closed her eyes. Zan's old bitterness must be showing. The lines on the old lady's forehead were spelling pain.

So Zan said, "You are right, Gran. It's better *not* to pry into old sorrows."

The old lady opened her eyes, and Zan received the glow of her affection. "Zan, dear, I am glad to see you. I always am. I'll be very glad when you move and are nearer to me."

Zan melted. She kissed the old lady's hairline and said, "Me, too, luv," and waltzed away.

Mrs. Moffat put her book aside, but lay in the lamplight remembering. This always had to happen when Zan came. Just once, or at least once, Mrs. Moffat had to review it. Odd, but each year the story seemed to change, just a little.

Begin with the week that Cynthia (suddenly in the hospital in Chicago) had roused herself a little late to let her in-laws know she was dying. Go on to the consultations after her funeral with social workers and psychological counselors and the Police. Tommy Moffat, aged fourteen, was hostile, sly, charming, shrewd, and totally slippery. Already a hardened delinquent, he had a long list of offenses on record.

His grandparents had taken expert advice. Tommy went into a special institution for special help. They paid his bills. It had been the right thing to do.

When he turned sixteen, the recommendation was that he go to a foster family—trained to this sort of thing—

and a public high school. His grandparents had gone to see him at that time and had found him much subdued and (on the surface) one who had seen the light and was resolved to enter into the straight and narrow and "work hard" and "be a success" within society's rules.

He had indeed rushed through high school at a fast rate (Tommy wasn't stupid) and had entered a small college in southern Wisconsin. The Moffats, of course, paid his tuition and his living expenses. All had seemed well.

Then a blow had fallen on Marguerite Moffat. Gerard had done her the discourtesy to die. He had left her alone to struggle to learn to live *at all* there for a while. (*I've learned,* she thought grimly.)

Now she must remember Tommy's flying visit—oh, not for his grandfather's funeral, but during the summer between his freshman and sophomore years. He had been well behaved and persuasive. He had convinced her (she might not have been thinking very clearly at that time) that the funds carefully designated by her husband's will for Tommy's higher education need not be doled out year by year but could be turned over to him *in toto,* then and there.

He had seemed resolved to be responsible; to do this would challenge him to be responsible, wouldn't it? She had agreed, and so it was done.

But before the fall semester was half over, Tommy Moffat had eloped with Alexandra Terry—he at the age of twenty; she, away from home for the first time in her life, aged sixteen. His letter—Mrs. Moffat still had it somewhere—had argued that life was the thing, not lore, and the two of them could lick the world anyhow, just as they were. There was nothing that she could do about this. So she had done nothing.

A year later, on one rainy morning, here came a battered old car, and here came Tommy Moffat and his seventeen-year-old very pregnant wife, whom Mrs. Moffat then met for the first time.

And here came, when the fluster of surprise and the welcoming of travelers was over, the appeal.

It did seem that Tommy had tried very hard in several

jobs, in several fields, to find the way that he should go to be husband and father, responsible citizen and success. But for one reason or another, nothing had really worked out, and in the meantime, the college money had gone. Well, yes, all of it, well, there were two of them, and Tommy had wanted darling Zan to be comfortable, naturally.

Mrs. Moffat remembered his face, the sly, the shrewd, the charming face, as he told her the rest of it. The fact was he had taken a sum of money out of the till of his latest employer. He'd been going to put it back, but the fact was right now the cops seemed to be after him, and Tommy didn't want to go to jail, and he was sure Gran wouldn't want him to go to jail either, so they had come to beg her to give him the money (it was gone, of course) so that he could give it back to his employer and thus escape very much and perhaps any punishment. Zan, poor little Zan, swallowed up in Tommy's philosophy, loving and torn and bound she'd be loyal to the dream, and swollen with child and shivering with terror and strain, had begged Mrs. Moffat to save them because he'd never do it again. He'd promised.

Mrs. Moffat skipped very fast over the next part. She had said *No*. She had said, *Certainly not*. She had said that if Tommy were a thief, he must take the consequences. She had said she took no stock in his promises. He himself had destroyed his credit. But—oh, how righteously, she had declaimed this part of it—she would in all human compassion see to it that this poor, cold, and bedraggled darling of his was taken care of. When had Alexandra last seen a decent doctor? How soon was the baby predicted? Mrs. Moffat would put her to bed *immediately*.

As for the authorities (the cops), Mrs. Moffat would not go so far as to summon them. But if they were to arrive, Mrs. Moffat would let them in and tell them honestly all that she knew.

So a terrible day, the rain continuing, the doctor coming, and Zan with a fever, and Polly running up and down the stairs, and Mrs. Moffat in a turmoil, and Tommy very quiet. A shadow in the house. Subdued. Saying nothing.

The next morning he had gone off to buy Zan a toothbrush—so he had said.

He had never come back.

In seven years, now—and a little more—Tommy had not been heard from.

It had taken three more days for Mrs. Moffat to discover how he had forged a withdrawal slip and taken away with him the bulk of her savings account.

Without a word. Without a word.

So Mrs. Moffat had been left, aged sixty-seven, with the hysterical, shattered, almost mortally wounded, outraged seventeen-year-old mother-to-be.

Had fed her and sheltered and dosed her and had waited in grim patience until the baby had been born dead, and that part of it was over. Then waited out more time, helpless to be anything but patient. Patient by default, she'd been. What else could she have done but wait for the screaming fits to lose some energy, suffering the accusations, "hard, cold, mean, evil," until they, too, began to die away? Waiting, saying very little. What could she have said? Tommy had done what he had done, stolen, and stolen again, and run away. Without a word, without a word for his beloved—and no query, even in the mail—nothing . . . nothing. No interest taken in the birth or death of his own child.

Zan at last had begun to pull herself together.

When Zan had one day written to her own people— something she had not been able to do heretofore—she had said to her husband's grandmother that she appreciated what had been given her here, but she was okay now. She would go home. She would be all right— probably.

Mrs. Moffat had seen in those sullen eyes that this girl was beginning to try to cast out of her crippled spirit all those accusations and the blame she had been forced to put somewhere handy.

And from her own spirit Mrs. Moffat had tried to cast

out her more or less hidden anger at such a little *fool* but had let her go, not without relief at that time.

But time changes, behind you. It is not true to say that the past can never change.

Tommy had not been a whole person, not ever. To ask him to be responsible was to ask the impossible. He was not now as cruel as he used to be in the story. Mrs. Moffat had made judgments that did not now seem to have been her own; she'd stood outside the character in the story who'd worn her name.

Mrs. Moffat *really* should have called the authorities, should have put before them Tommy's record, should have brought in those who had treated Tommy, should have told all the truth she knew. And not in panic run to righteous compromise. Or taken on that mad and maddening girl, to be martyred, stubborn, not understanding why *she* needed punishment.

Now, looking back, that hard, furious contempt for an Alexandra Terry who (formerly) had thrown her life away and wrecked it forever, just to lie in Tommy Moffat's arms, had been a blindness. Mrs. Moffat could see that her own Zan—so strong and bright and independent—had been there all the time, and by luck—by luck—had not been let to die. Ah, well, the color of old sorrows could change as well as fade.

Zan put out her lamp, looked out the window for a moment, at the low roof of the one-story portion of the house, at the blot of the great tree that interrupted the patterns of the stars. She couldn't see the wing of the garage they called the cottage, where there was a man who had once known Tommy Moffat.

She crept into bed and (as she always must, at least once, when she came here) began to live through the whole thing again.

Oh, that *heaven!* That heavenly hell-bent recklessness. The knowing—the knowing—the knowing that this was all ... This was ALL! And nothing else could possibly matter but their bodies together! She cringed and squirmed between the cold sheets. All right, that was gone. All right.

And then the pell-mell quality of the downhill race. She couldn't have stopped it. No one could have stopped it. Tommy was hell-bent. That was a good word for him.

She remembered the long flight across the continent in the old car, the fever and strain. Then, in the cold rain, this house, and how even then she had thought it was old, and the old woman, sexless and unfeeling—and all the hot drinks and the hot-water bottles and the blankets and the pillows had counted for nothing because there was still only one thing that really mattered. And oh, if they came and took Tommy . . . All right. That was over.

So—the next morning, waking alone in the big bed in the other bedroom, the other front one (Zan never went in there) and Tommy's grandmother coming with a tray, asking how she felt, and Zan sure *she* couldn't care, but answering the question with pleading softness. Oh, save us yet?

Skip to the night. Heart in her mouth. Where? Dark again, and he hadn't come. He had gone to hide then, from the cops? He would send for her. There would be some secret way that he would send the word.

Waiting. Oh, damn the baby! Once she got the baby out of her and was herself, *then* he would send for them.

Travail and the news that the baby was not going to have to be reared. So she had shaken off that crushed and cheated feeling. But this meant when he sent for her, she would be light of foot to go.

Shaken it *off?* Zan skipped on.

So sometimes she had eaten what his grandmother said she ought to eat, seeking strength. But sometimes she had felt so lost and so cruelly deprived that she *must* scream.

But slowly, slowly, at first in short flashes and then in longer stretches of time, she had been able to get it plain. Tommy was gone. Tommy would be free; so he had abandoned her. He would never send. He did not have the persistence; he would not pick up his obligations or act to undo what once was done.

Okay, Zan told herself, *now you've been through that again. So shut up and go to sleep.*

Zan turned over and thought to herself that Mrs. Moffat was only up to her old tricks, after all. She could well remember (when she dared try) herself, aged seventeen, all in pieces, frantic, perhaps insane, half in her grave, and how by persistent, obstinate, steady, unconquerable, and perfectly *routine* nonintrusive kindness, she had been coaxed or led the way to life. Now, if Gran was trying such old tricks on this strange young man with the weird beard, wasn't Zan the last person—

A thought came and struck her with such force that she sat up in bed, heart racing, pain pounding in her head. *What* was hidden under that beard? Scars, from some kind of surgery? Had that man been somehow smashed and patched up, and was his memory in patches, too? *Was that man Tommy Moffat?*

Oh, no, no! Not Tommy's bones. Tommy's hair, all of it, everywhere, had been black. Oh, God, she knew that very well. Oh, God! Zan settled back, bathed in sweat now, to wait out the shock.

Tommy is dead, she thought grimly. *I've seen to that.*

Then crept the old longing for the redemption she once feared and sometimes prayed for. What if he had died, some sudden way, *before* he could send for her? Suppose this Simon knew?

"So what?" the man said stormily. "I'm telling you now. And that's more than the old bitch has done, or darling Zan either. She's my wife. Established and prosperous, eh? I'd like to know what the hell she ever did with the kid! That's what I'd like to know. Listen, Al. The people who live in the Warrens' house. Find out how much longer they'll be away."

"Why?" said the red-bearded boy.

"Because something's coming out of this. Don't ask me what. I've got a feeling—I've got to find out about—oh statutes—yah."

He walked the short length of the room, limping badly. He had a full black beard now. It was unkempt. His right eye was excited. His left eye looked, in the flesh, as if it were part of a knot in a tree over which the bark was growing in rolls that might soon meet and close.

He was dirty, and he stank, and he said, "Wouldn't my seven-year-old kid be tickled to death to meet old Dad? I wonder what my darling Zan would say to that?"

The red-bearded boy said nothing, but the black-bearded man changed tone at once. "Listen," he said. "I've got to eat. I don't think she would refuse me a little allowance. She can afford it, wouldn't you say?"

"I guess so," muttered the boy.

Chapter 7

WHEN Mrs. Moffat came down the next morning, Simon was already at work on the back border, where he was proposing to set some bright hibiscus once the soil was ready. Zan, up almost as early as he, on New York time, was prowling the downstairs rooms, peering at old pieces of furniture, assessing their condition and period, testing the state of her professional knowledge. (Zan did this every time she came.) And all day Mrs. Moffat's two young guests seemed to be going their ways within their separate interests, one outdoors, one indoors, not interested in each other particularly.

Still, Mrs. Moffat could sense a turbulence. *Perhaps it's Zan,* she thought. The girl had the gift and the habit of energy. She was accustomed to running very fast, all day, every day. Zan was not one to surrender, relax where she was, sit and absorb. The pace in this house was much too slow for her. (*And should be,* her grandmother thought.)

Simon took his lunch apart in his working clothes, and when he came for Mrs. Moffat so that they could walk their rounds for that day, Zan was buried in contemplation of some ormolu in the parlor and declined to join them.

Mrs. Moffat was just as glad.

This separation could not last, of course. So, Mrs. Moffat having warned Zan, thought now that she might warn Simon. She said to him, "Zan comes from the world; she thrives in the thick of it, so she brings a kind of turbulence. Whenever she comes, I must always learn again how very much out of the world I am. I must say," she added, "I wind up feeling darned glad of it."

"Yes, ma'am," he said. "Excuse me, Mrs. Moffat, but is she *Mrs.* Terry?"

Mrs. Moffat's heart jumped. (Well, she wouldn't lie.)

"No, she's really Mrs. Moffat. She was Tommy's wife."

"Why didn't you tell me?" he said in a minute, with more curiosity than shock.

"Because we don't speak of old, unhappy things," she said sternly. "And it really doesn't matter anymore."

"Weren't there any children?"

She looked at his face. His eyes were squinted up as if to keep secrets.

"The baby never lived," she said. She thought, *Did its father care enough to mention it?* She discovered that *she* did not care in the least anymore whether Tommy Moffat had ever mentioned the baby. What bothered her was a certain turbulence present here in her garden.

But Simon, peering into the greenery, said cheerfully, "Aren't the neighbors ever coming home?"—changing the subject and the mood, sounding much happier.

"Not till Labor Day," said Mrs. Moffat absently. Thinking to herself how disjointed were the bits and pieces of information one received. Why should the death of Zan's baby, seven years ago, make Simon happier? Something must be missing.

When she came indoors, Mrs. Moffat had a very strong intuition that Zan had only just now rustled away from a window. Ah, well—curiosity was only natural.

While Mrs. Moffat was resting, Zan slipped outdoors to say hello to her grandmother's hired gardener. Ben Guest was in a dour mood. He kept darting dour glances at the far figure of Simon.

"I see you have some help around here," said Zan gaily.

Ben burst into passionate speech. "He don't know what he's doing, and she don't either. Too much upkeep, *she's* going to find out. And I can't put even a foot in the cottage. 'No more,' she says."

"Oh."

"He's got her wrapped around his pinky, and who does he think he is—red-headed ape! Darn *kid!*"

Zan, as soon as she could, went indoors, somewhat dismayed.

Toward evening, when Simon joined them on the porch where Polly was setting the glass-topped summery table, all three settled in their chairs, and it should have been, Mrs. Moffat thought, as the day was sifting down to dark, and all its dust behind it, a time for placid reflections. But Zan began to worry and push at the question of the car.

"Is there any day when I could have it, Gran, and not discommode you?" asked Zan, her pretty legs twined together tensely, her face animated, her attractive mouth moving in fascinating ways. "I'm going to have to run around seeing people, and that's the only way to get around in these parts, isn't that so? I can rent a car, of course."

Mrs. Moffat said reluctantly, "I suppose we could plan." She didn't want to plan; she didn't want to decide just what errands must be done at just what hour. But she roused herself.

Zan said, "I don't mean tomorrow. I'll have to get on the horn tomorrow and poke up my contacts. Maybe I could squash all my appointments into say a couple of days. But I'll have to run around looking at locations, *too*."

Mrs. Moffat sighed. "Why don't you make your arrangements, Zan, and let me know?"

Zan was wearing sandals. Mrs. Moffat saw her bare toes convulse.

"You're getting it backward, Gran," she said. "I thought I was just asking *you* to let *me* know. Wasn't I, Simon?"

Simon was looking at her out of his eye corners. "I couldn't say," he murmured.

Mrs. Moffat brought her mind to the problem and said, "Now tomorrow, I must go for my checkup to Dr. Sebastian. What could we combine? If I drop you at the nursery, Simon, could you just as well—"

"No, no," Zan broke in. "If you're going to the doctor's, Gran, you are *not* driving yourself. I'll take you, and drop Simon wherever he needs to be dropped and pick him up afterward." She turned abruptly to Simon. "A pity you can't drive. You could have been useful all this while, couldn't you?" She flashed a big and obviously phony smile.

Simon said, slumberously, "I can drive. Mrs. Moffat enjoys to do what she can do."

"I see," Zan said, eyes wide. "Of course, if she were to get used to a chauffeur, she'd be awfully out of practice by the time you went away, wouldn't she?"

He seemed not to have heard this. "Don't you feel well, ma'am?"

"I hope," said Mrs. Moffat haughtily, "that I have sense enough to know when I don't feel well enough to go to the doctor."

Zan looked at her and let out a whoop of laughter.

But Simon had turned his head away and was looking at the trees.

"You may drive me tomorrow, Zan," said Mrs. Moffat as benignly as she could manage, "but I think, after that, you must just take the car whenever you need it. Simon and Polly and I can make do with the intervals. We are flexible."

"We don't have to run around particularly," said Simon lazily.

Zan seemed not to have heard this.

Mrs. Moffat did the best she could to preen herself at table, arguing that this was delightful, two such handsome young people and both her friends. But she was suffering a revival of an old uneasiness, that of the inexperienced hostess who has brought together friends of hers who are not yet friends to one another. This was described fairly well by the image of a chameleon on a swatch of plaid. She was one thing to Simon and another to Zan. Nonsense. Mrs. Moffat had gone past such foolishness, surely. She was the real thing in a grown-up, was she not? One who spoke and acted from her own core at all times.

All very well for theory, but in practice one is many-sided, and how did one show two equally genuine but different sides at once?

Zan chattered on about her work, her imminent trans-fer, the problems involved, and Mrs. Moffat couldn't help hearing the overtones of her energy, her competitive drive, her worldly wisdom, her slightly cynical tolerance for her clients, and her caustic humor. Zan was sounding merely *busy*.

Inevitably she turned the talk to Simon and began to worry and push for some definition of *his* ambition.

"If you want to be a gardener, how do you get to be one?" she inquired. "Must you be apprenticed, or something? Are there schools?"

Mrs. Moffat said, as far as she knew, you took your courage in your hands and simply announced that you *were* a gardener. Then, of course, you had to prove it. She thought that Simon was uneasy.

"You ought to take up landscaping. There must be courses," Zan went on. "It should be fascinating to design whole vistas, to arrange the scene to suit the eye, to take a piece of land and form the plantings in dimension."

Zan was using her hands to show her sense of power. Simon was giving her his owl stare. "Prestige, if you're good enough to please the 'in' group," she said as if she were promising sugar plums. "There's serious money to be made."

"There is?" he drawled, startling Mrs. Moffat with a voice for Zan she'd never heard before.

"Surely you wouldn't mind?" drawled Zan.

"I've been away," he said. "I guess I forgot what we are all here for."

"You are not *that* ambitious?" said Zan kindly.

"Well, it was more that I like being outdoors, you see."

Mrs. Moffat, who had long ago given up any belief that fame and fortune were plausible human goals, since in her opinion, they always covered for something else, said placatingly, "The two of you are not alike, Zan. You are busy climbing up the ladder. But Simon's going the other way."

Simon met her eyes, and his were smiling. She had not said exactly what she meant, but he knew what she meant, just the same. She felt a wave of comfort.

"Whatever that means." Zan shrugged. She had no clue to Simon's side of Mrs. Moffat. "Of course, money isn't good for much," she went on, "unless you figure to pay

your board and room with it, and things like that." She
gave Simon another phony smile and spooned her dessert.

"Some people can learn a good deal," said Mrs.
Moffat, "given the peace to do it."

Zan flushed.

Ah, well, when children are naughty, you must spank,
in Mrs. Moffat's philosophy.

Simon was looking puzzled now.

Mrs. Moffat sighed within and took over the table talk,
balancing as best she could among her selves.

When at last they left the table, Zan walked close to
the screen to gaze out at the sunset's reflection in the eastern sky.

Simon stood politely waiting for Mrs. Moffat to seat
herself, and just as the hostess did so, Zan whirled around
suddenly. "Tell me, Simon, are you planning to be the
local handyman in that beard?"

It was as if she had turned up under his nose, she stood
so close. "If that's a disguise," she went on saucily, "it's
pretty darned spectacular. As a matter of fact, it's gor-
geous." Her right hand moved. "Is it soft?"

He startled like a woodsy creature. "Get away."

"Sit down, Zan," Mrs. Moffat said, "and stop being so
naughty."

"Well, I'm sure I'm very *sorry*," said Zan in tones of
complete surprise at such an accusation. She skirted with
elaborate avoidance Simon *and* his chair and folded herself into a leggy heap on the settee. Oh, she'd been
naughty, and still was. The turbulence was made of
sparks and arcings.

Mrs. Moffat said sternly, "Sit down, Simon, do," and
then she launched into the long saga of a certain hum-
mingbird who had used to live here. It lasted four minutes.
The two of them waited it out. Then Simon begged to be,
and was, excused.

As soon as he had gone, Mrs. Moffat rose and went
into the house.

She knew that Zan was following; she wished she
didn't have to scold; she wished she didn't have to talk at
all.

Zan said, "Oooo, I betcha I'm going to catch it." She spoke with that air she had sometimes, half repentance and half mischief. "I shouldn't have mentioned his precious beard."

"No, you should not have," said Mrs. Moffat. *As if that's all you did,* she thought.

"But didn't he have a strange reaction?"

"Not at all," said Mrs. Moffat, sitting down.

"Gran," said Zan earnestly, sitting down at her feet, "I do understand you, I do. You think he needs a little quiet kindness, and you are probably right. The only thing that bothers me, how come he's got you so sold on the idea that nobody asks *him* any questions? If he can drive, why doesn't he? If only sometimes? And if he has got something wrong with his memory, why can't he just say so?"

"Alexandra," Mrs. Moffat said, "I thought I had suggested to you—"

"I know you did," wailed Zan. "But, Gran—luv . . . How much do you know about that man? *Anything?* Except that he was once the next-door child. And you won't ask and you won't let me ask," Zan went on. "I can't understand what he's up to. Why does he hang on here, all this time?"

"Perhaps he enjoys himself here," said Mrs. Moffat loftily. "I have enjoyed having him—up to now."

"All right," said Zan. "So you've gotten fond of him and he *is* just as sweet as he can be—to *you.* But one of these days when he asks you to make some investments, don't sign the papers."

"Really, Zan. I have been dealing with financial matters quite a few years longer than you."

"Okay, but if you even suggest that there might be something wrong with his mind—"

"I told you that I believe he has seen some trouble," said Mrs. Moffat, "as who has not."

"Wouldn't it make a little difference what kind of trouble?" said Zan coaxingly.

"I don't quite see why." Mrs. Moffat was beginning to feel stubborn.

"But, Gran, supposing he ran away, for instance, from some mental institution? You never know, these days."

Mrs. Moffat thought crossly, These *days*, these *days, they are not the only days the world has seen or ever will see.*

"I daresay it seems insane these days," she said, "that a young man rather enjoys being the guest of an old woman."

"All right, Gran," said Zan softly in a moment. "I don't want to get into a fight. But please be sensible a minute. Isn't it true that you don't know one darned thing about him? Where he's been for how many years? What is on his mind, or the real reason that he—well, settles for puttering around your backyard at his age? Has it occurred to you that this is a pretty snug harbor and a pretty cute hiding place, for that matter?"

"It has occurred to me," said Mrs. Moffat stiffly.

"Well?"

"He doesn't hide, Zan. He goes where he pleases."

"How do you know where he pleases to go? What if the law is after him? *That's* what's under the beard? He could have escaped from jail, for all you know."

"Why escaped?" said Mrs. Moffat. "He may have been in prison somewhere and been let out."

"What do you mean?"

Mrs. Moffat didn't answer. She had meant "Does no one ever get forgiven? Does no one ever outlive trouble? Didn't you?"

She didn't speak.

"Don't you see?" Zan wheedled. "All I'm trying to say is that he just might be dangerous, and I don't like—"

"Can't you let us be, Zan?" said Mrs. Moffat wearily.

"But I can't help wondering," said Zan. "You are pretty much all alone, Gran—and you *are* more vulnerable than you probably realize. I'm sure that you do enjoy having him at your beck and call, so devoted and so polite and all. But it just can't be."

"Can't be what?"

"It just can't be that simple," said Zan, "or that innocent."

Mrs. Moffat was good and mad now, and knew this very well. Detached from the anger, a part of her considered whether or not to give way to it. She compromised.

"Dear me," she said, in a voice that betrayed no anger, "since I am nearly finished, I supposed I ought to cherish my wrinkled hide unto the bitter end."

"Oh, Gran!"

But Mrs. Moffat went on without mercy. "The only desirable way to die, for instance, is to do it as slowly, as draggingly, as *boringly* as possible. But why is that, I wonder? Why is it that I, being seventy-four years old, may not run the risk of having any fun? Any fun, anymore?"

Zan buried her head in her arms. "Don't—"

"You fancy that Simon Warren is going to hurt me somehow? Is that inevitable? Do you know, Zan, it sounds too *simple* to me."

"Won't you be hurt already," said Zan in a muffled voice, "when he goes away?"

"Not as much as you think," said her grandmother. "I am better prepared for partings and departings than you imagine. I appreciate your concern. I understand that you mean well—"

"You sure know how to hurt a guy," said Zan, raising her head. "I was only trying to use good sense."

"Yes," said Mrs. Moffat. "Ah, well, if Simon is gone in the morning, as he very well may be, without even saying good-bye, that will have been the consequence of your . . . good sense, do you say?"

"All right, I was mad at you," said Zan. "Or jealous. Or something stupid. Or as annoyed as hell with him, sitting there like a big old ginger cat and lapping up the cream. Besides, I didn't like the way you put *me* out. What did you *mean*—going the other way? I couldn't make any sense of that. What is the other way? *Down* the ladder?"

"I could try to tell you," said Mrs. Moffat, "if I weren't so tired." She began to struggle out of her chair, and Zan rose quickly and hooked her young arm under Mrs. Moffat's.

"Don't do that," said the old lady crossly. "It doesn't help. Simon *never* does that."

"No, he doesn't, does he?" murmured Zan, stepping away. "He keeps his paws to himself, I'll say that for him."

Mrs. Moffat was on her feet. "You may hand me my cane," she said sternly. "This kind of turbulence tires me very much, Alexandra. Too much. I didn't mean going *down* the ladder," she went on to her own surprise. "But I can't explain to you a world with no ladder in it, can I? So I'll forgive you, and go to bed with my book, and to sleep when I feel like it, and I'll wake when I wake. And if I were as wise as I sometimes seem to sound, I would now shut my mouth and say no more."

Zan kissed her.

Toiling up the stairs, Mrs. Moffat tried to feel resigned. *Zan will drive him away,* she thought. *Perhaps that's best.*

Zan listened anxiously to the old lady's progress. Mrs. Moffat did not like to be helped, enjoyed to do what she was able. Zan had known that for years. Ah, she was a *dear* and a darling, this old lady, but damned exasperating. Involved now where she must be misreading the signs, flattered and eagerly mistaken ... so easily fooled by a young man, with the power of that one.

She went to turn off the downstairs lights, all but one in the sitting room. She stepped out onto the wide porch into the night air. It was early. They had dined just before sundown. Simon had left them very soon thereafter. Zan and her grandmother had argued as the dark came swiftly down. It was not really bedtime yet.

Zan went to the screen door and opened it without making a sound. She stepped outside and coaxed the door to settle behind her in the same furtive way. Polly had finished in the kitchen; she must be in her room. No one could see. Zan walked on the grass, avoiding the gravel path until she had to take the narrow one that led through a leafy tunnel to the cottage door.

There was light in the cottage window. But no light fell

where Zan stood at the door, in deep dark, listening. There was no sound. Yet the crunch of her feet must have been loud. The whole night held its breath. Zan had a strong sense of fate. She was doomed to do what she was now about to do. She tapped. Simon's voice said at once, "Who is it?"

"Alexandra Terry. May I please talk to you for a minute?"

Silence. Then the window to her left went black. The door opened, and he stepped from darkness out into darkness. He wasn't going to let her in.

"I've upset Gran," she said quickly, "so I've come to apologize to you and ask you not—"

"About this beard," he said in no gentle voice. "Sure it's a disguise." He sagged against the cottage wall. "What do you want?" he snarled. "See, probably after I beat her up and take all her *money,* then I'll shave. And you'll never catch me."

Zan said coldly, "Do you mind not being silly? The point is, because I was rude, she's afraid you'll vanish without saying good-bye. That would break her heart, so please—"

"It wouldn't dent yours any," he barked. "I'll go when she says to go, and she knows it. So don't you fret your little head about me not saying good-bye."

"Are you sure she ever *will* say to go?" breathed Zan. "As long as you mind your manners with *her*, haven't you got it made?"

"What do you want?" he said roughly. "You're so damned sure I'm going to break her heart, or else her neck, you can't wait to boot me out of here. What do you want, Mrs. Moffat?"

"Since you ask," said Zan, bracing, "I want to know just when you last saw Tommy Moffat."

"*You'd* break her heart. Oh, you'd do it in a minute," he cried in a rush, as if anger had carried him over her question and kept him from hearing it. "Get away," he growled. "Get away."

"Oh, listen, listen," cried Zan, casting off the hostility that she knew very well to be a kind of sex play anyhow.

"You can't blame me for wanting to know what you're up to. I only want to understand—" She reached to touch him.

He jumped away in the dark; she knew it. Then the dark was singing with a thousand messages, pulse to pulse, across the little distance.

"Some people can't have what they want," he said harshly. "Ever hear of bad luck like that?"

"What's the matter?" said Zan quietly. She was remembering that he hadn't even shaken hands. He never touched her grandmother to help her on their rounds. "Are you untouchable or something?"

"Why do you ask questions?" he said in bitter fury, "when you couldn't take the answers? Stick to your decorating, city girl. What do you know about the world?"

Still he loomed in the dark. She couldn't breathe.

He said, "Do you have to make trouble?" His breath rasped. He broke all invisible links and bonds and ran. He had not opened the cottage door. He was gone on the path, loose in the dark. She'd never catch him.

Zan waited until the silence seemed to have sealed over the shock of the encounter. Then she trudged slowly the way back to the safe house.

Safe? She wondered. Within the walls, inside the charming sitting room, where all her grandmother's things soaked in bygone graces, the raw anguish, the throb of desperate trouble in that man seemed outrageous.

I can't let Gran keep him here, Zan thought. *I just can't. She'll never boot him out, so I'll have to do it, somehow. Oh, he's dangerous.*

She thought there must be some terrible split within the man, as if he had been riven by lightning; the torn halves would crash like thunder if ever they came together.

For herself, she was not afraid. Zan recognized a temptation toward excitement. (She couldn't afford it, of course.) But the dear old lady, so innocently kind, so long shut away from worldly peril—evil passions ... so fragile now ...

She made her brain begin to analyze the problem. Zan must protect her.

DEAR SMITTY:
  How are you?

The hand put down the pencil and picked up the can of beer. The hand put down the can and picked up the pencil and blacked out the three words, so savagely as to tear the paper.

  You know what they did . . [The pencil scurried.] You know how they wiped me out like chalk from a blackboard? Well, it's as if she's got the chalk in her hand and she's making a picture, and it isn't me or it isn't you—but it's what *she* should have had for a grandson—and I'm sorry if it's not true. I wish good things could be true. They can't even be half-true, now that your wife's here.
  Busy, busy, busy, busy . . .

The pencil began to make great loops and scribbles all over the writing.

DEAR SMITTY:
  The baby didn't live. Listen, we can try and get hold of a car, make a down payment of a few bucks and sign away three or four years. So who cares? We can start south, just the same, and take our chances. I can't stay here much longer. Only buy the medicine. Will you *please* buy the medicine?

Chapter 8

THE next morning, Wednesday, Mrs. Moffat was relieved to see Simon grubbing away in the borders as usual, and to find Zan taking up the position of disinterested separation again.

Zan, chattering away about everything else but Simon, drove her to the doctor's and to market. Since Simon (taking up the position of disinterested separation, too?) had said, "There isn't any hurry about the shrubs, is there, ma'am?" and watched her lips, as if he were lip reading, as well as listening, when she said, "Well, of course not."

Disinterested separation between one's guests, however, is not the most comfortable position in the world for the hostess, and when Zan had gone off on her dinner date, Mrs. Moffat felt herself letting down from tension.

Come now, this is too bad, she thought. *Zan is my darling.*

The mysterious thing was that Polly served her mistress and Simon Warren their evening meal in a state of anxiety that amounted to the jitters. This wasn't mysterious very long to Mrs. Moffat, who could not help feeling sad. How cruel of Zan, how destructive to Polly—that the old cook should have been warned to watch over her mistress lest the guest begin to be troublesome.

She did what she could about it, continuing to be kind and easy. It was not until after dinner that she could let down. Into old times, new times, times stolen from the stern sequence of hours, times that would be lost and past, one day, and soon.

Nicky had chosen a restaurant on the shore. They sat at the window and could see the broad flat tongues of the waves' tips licking the floodlit sand below. In the semi-dark beyond, the breakers curled and tossed like the manes of white horses. Sometimes, in the foreground, a bird walked daintily by.

The food had been so-so. Now Nicky was drawing a ticktacktoe design on the tablecloth with his coffee spoon. He said, "Aren't you in too much of a flap, Zan? Say this character wants to strangle your grandmother? He's had six weeks to do it, hasn't he? *Has* he?"

"Well, no," said Zan, reasonably.

Nicky liked the way she looked; he liked the way she held her head, the way she used her pretty hands. Her luscious mouth, distinctive, he liked very much. The news that she was moving out here was too interesting to discuss.

He said, "I'm not crazy about your only solution."

"What is that?" she asked, tilting her head, smiling with her eyes, lifting her pretty hands, in question. "I wasn't so sure I had one."

"Simple elimination. Can't say she's senile and take over yourself?"

"Not a chance," she said. "Dr. Sebastian laughed and laughed."

"Can't throw him out for a trespasser either?"

"Not when he's a guest."

"If he's got a swindle in mind, you don't know what it is. Correct?"

"Nothing showing."

"Can't make your grandmother shiver and shake. She won't scare, eh?"

"She'll never scare," said Zan, sighing. "She more or less claims to be expendable. That's how scared she is. I haven't even tried to tell her the way he talked to me."

Nicky thought, *Of course not. You don't want her to know what you do behind her back. Talk to her doctor; beard Simon in his den.* Nicky couldn't blame this.

"She'd never believe it," Zan said.

"So," Nicky said, "the only way to put the fellow off the property is for you to be such a stinker that he can't stand to be where you are."

"It would seem so," said Zan calmly. "But what's to stop him from running back when *I've* gone away, to pack and all?"

"You say the old lady is having a ball?"

"Oh, yes."

"Then let her alone, why don't you?"

"And when he does get around to strangling her, I can always say, 'So? That's the way it goes, sometimes.' " Zan gave an exaggerated shrug.

"She's right about one thing. It *is* her neck."

"Damn it," said Zan. "Don't you know old people can be as ornery as babies? So you'll let your kid take poison because it's *his* stomach!"

Nicky scratched his chin. "It's also *her* money. You know how this looks, don't you? Looks like you're scared she'll take a notion to change her will and the charming protégé will take it all."

"For God's sake, Nicky," Zan's back slapped the bench back, and her palms slapped the tabletop.

"And you won't do yourself any good," he continued, "because if you do act the stinker and chase him off, she's not going to like that, and you could be out of the money anyhow."

"What if I don't particularly insist I've got to be *in* the money?" she said icily.

"Oh, that's right," he said. "It was her neck, wasn't it? Not that you wanted to run her life or anything?"

Zan didn't take offense. She settled somehow, cocked her head, and spoke quietly. "Nicky, am I one of those obnoxious, aggressive, domineering females? Am I that bad?"

"Why do you ask?" he evaded.

"Because I've been catching it ever since I came. Gran says I boss people around. You've been sending me the same message; so I seem to hear. Even Simple Simon, in his simplicity—"

"Well," said Nicky, "after all, there they were, having a happy time, and here comes Zan, and right away she's bound she'll bust it up—or know the reason why."

"Don't I have a reason?"

"Suspicion. Speculation. Probability. I guess they are forms of reason." Nicky could be icy, too.

Zan said, clasping her hands under her chin and looking straight at him, "It could be you have a point, Nicky. How can I go about some fact finding? How can I get onto traces of this Simon Warren? If he *has* been in jail, or if he *is* wanted, or if he *was* recently in a mental hospital, then it wouldn't quite seem a compulsion inherent in my nasty personality, would it? Do you have a way?"

"No, not especially," said Nicky. He ran, although he did not own, a research service for motion-picture and TV producers. He had a staff trained to answer millions of questions of fact, and Zan knew it. "For that you'd need a private eye," he said uneasily.

"But I had understood," purred Zan, "that you do hunt down facts for a fee?"

"Sure, sure, I can find out what an Eskimo has for breakfast. It'll cost you." Nicky was accepting the check from the little tray and fishing for his wallet.

"Gran says he was in the service, but she doesn't know which branch. Can't you trace a man through the Red Cross? Do you have to hire a PI?"

Nicky said, "Tell you what would be a whole lot cheaper. Ask old Simple Simon."

"Okay," said Zan cheerfully. "I'll ask him whether he intends to strangle my grandmother, and he'll say 'Why, yes, of course.' And then I'll know."

"Ask him was he in the Army," said Nicky patiently. "Is that a thing one keeps to oneself?"

"In the first place, Gran forbids me to ask him."

"Oh, well, then——" He grinned at her.

"In the second place," she went on, "he doesn't have to answer me, truthfully or at all, and also it's possible he can't answer."

"Why not?"

"Because he may not know himself."

"You mean he's some kind of kook?"

"Oh, *that* he is," she said. "Some kind."

"In *your* opinion," said Nicky. "All God's children got

opinions, and one man's kook is another man's saintly hero. If you say he is a kook, although no harm's been done, watch out you don't promote any, I'd say."

"I'd thought of that," said Zan clearly.

"I've got a little question for you," he went on silky-voiced. "Are we going to my place?"

"I had thought so," she smiled.

"Are we going to talk about this Simple Simon the whole night?"

"Are you by any chance or-elsing me, darling?"

"I'm hinting," he said gloomily. "I'm hinting."

Afterward they sat in Nicky's huge twin easy chairs and stared out over the twinkling city. Nicky was holding her in the corners of his eyes. He was thinking about marriage, but although he was pretty sure she was thinking about it, too, it seemed too complex and cold-blooded a subject to bring up in the wake of so simple and warm an experience.

He knew when her thoughts drifted, when she was no longer seeing his fabulous view or holding him in the corners of her eyes or even in the corner of her mind.

Nicky was suddenly annoyed, as well as stricken, by a sense of omen.

"I'm taking you home now," he said abruptly. It was early by both their reckonings.

She looked up, startled.

"'Where the McGregor sits' and all that," he said. "Or if not, what then? I don't want to *discuss* it, mind you. I'd rather figure it out by myself."

"Me, too," she said, and rose with grace and smiled at him.

"We'll go sailing on Saturday," he decreed.

"Like Columbus," she promised.

Nicky began to believe that he could teach her, after all, or that a marriage between them might be just enough of a struggle for dominance to stay interesting.

They drove off toward her grandmother's house, seeming for some reason closer than before. When they got there, they kissed, and the kissing was sweet.

Zan got out of the car at last and turned and said, "Nicky, would you please come to supper Sunday night?"

"Here?" He was startled.

"For this reason," she spoke slowly. Her face was smooth and grave in the wan moonlight. "I was thinking, just before you snatched me by the hair of my head, and all, that I might be all wrong about my grandmother's protégé. He may be just a slightly Simple Simon, perfectly harmless. So—I'd like you to meet him."

"For what reason?" said Nicky.

"Because, since your opinions come in the package, I'd like to explore what they can do for me."

"That seems sensible," said Nicky.

He kissed her again and drove off, feeling quite pleased with himself. Halfway home it occurred to him that Zan had not (to his knowledge) bothered to ask the old lady whether Nicky could come to Sunday supper, that Nicky had not the slightest desire to take supper with the old lady at all and furthermore would much rather not be put on a spot where he'd have to make any informed recommendations in the matter of the mysterious protégé.

Well, well, Zan was a sweet young thing in many, many ways, but Nicky guessed she needed watching.

Zan came into the hall and saw that one lamp burned in the sitting room. Had it been left for her, she wondered, and was she supposed to put it out? She started into the long room, moving quietly, and then because the night was moon-whitened, she was able to see past the open double doors their silhouettes.

Against the pale light, she saw her grandmother's outline in the big rocker. Her shoulders muffled in her gray woolen stole, the knot on the top of her head, one hand moving as if she conducted slow music. She saw him in his own chair, round head, features blunted by the beard (Odysseus, come ashore!). He was immobile, either asleep (but she didn't think so) or intent to listen.

Zan felt that she had been jumped violently from one world to another. There was Nicky's high platform,

stacked upon nine other apartments of the identical design. Nine layers and a pavement between him and the
earth. A perch for bright-plumaged creatures, where they
could peck and preen, imprisoned in the glass.

Then this, no vista at all—hidden low, closed and
close-kept, sweet with the scent of living grass.

She didn't announce herself or interrupt them. She
crept back to the stairs and went up silently. In her room,
where the window was open, she could, by leaning on the
sill, catch the faintest murmur of voices. She couldn't
distinguish any words. She had a feeling that she couldn't
have understood them anyway. But the rhythms spoke to
her of something—illusive as the content of a dream that
you wish you could dream again, when only its healing
tone remains to haunt you in the morning.

Chapter 9

ON Thursday Zan asked humbly for the use of the car today, provided that this would inconvenience no one. She then asked if she might give a supper party Sunday evening, a party to which Mrs. Moffat must come. Zan would plan the menu, buy the food, and would her grandmother mind if she invited Nicky Pomerance? And Simon Warren, too?

"Of course I don't mind, dear. I can't speak for Simon."

"Then why don't I ask him?" Zan kicked off her shoes and went marching barefoot across the lawn. Mrs. Moffat was the one, this time, to lurk at a window.

She saw them speak. Then (to her pleasure) she saw Zan hold out her hand, and (to her surprise) she saw Simon, after rubbing his right hand down his pants leg and inspecting it, suddenly thrust it to the clasping.

Zan came swinging back. "The party's on. Now I've got to leap into my career girl costume."

She flew upstairs and shortly thereafter came down looking smart and went off in the car, saying she'd be back by dinnertime.

So the daytime hours fell into their undemanding pace, and Mrs. Moffat knew that she was glad of it.

As they went their rounds that day, Simon seemed diffident about the proposed new shrubs.

"Ma'am, you choose the colors," he said. "I won't be here when they bloom."

"They won't care," said Mrs. Moffat.

He gave her a sharp, quizzical look.

"They'll be fighting to thrive like everything else, and most people," she said. "They're ingenious, you know. They'll twist around in the strangest ways to find a place in the sun. Some plants will, that is. Of course, some are as sulky as a spoiled brat, and if everything isn't just so, they'll quit on you. They're difficult, so they're supposed to be precious. But I say, *they're* just in the wrong place. They'd probably be as common as weeds if they were where they ought to be. There's something to be said for the common weed, don't you think, Simon? Angels must be extremely common in heaven."

"Yes, ma'am," he said respectfully.

Mrs. Moffat felt along the grass with her cane and stepped after it. It was a bit of a shock to realize that she was in the moment perfectly happy. She was walking easily in the sun; the light itself was falling as soft as a mantle of kindly wool around her shoulders. Something was bubbling under her breastbone. It went through to the spine and upward, so that the whole back of her head seemed to have a song in it.

Why is this? she wondered, toning the lovely feeling down to hang on to it a little longer. Ah, well, she had been playing the wise old woman again. But it was such fun!

And since all human beings are bound to be wrong to some degree, at all times, why shouldn't Mrs. Moffat now and then have a little fun? She seemed to see the whole world—here and abroad—abounding with people telling other people in fine didactic sentences what the truth is, and not a one of them getting it exactly right. Not a one. Laughter bubbled along her breastbone.

They went past the old compost pit, deepened by Simon's digging, but still veiled by strands of ivy. They rounded the cottage corners. They drew opposite the empty garage. This was the place of parting. From here she would walk on alone to the house and upstairs for her nap.

"I was delighted, Simon," said Mrs. Moffat impulsively, "when I saw you and Zan shaking hands this morning."

"I wouldn't want to hurt anyone at all," he said startling her. He had turned up his palms and bent his bright head. Mrs. Moffat was sharply reminded of the stained-glass window. "I never want to hurt anybody, anywhere, anytime, ever again," he said as if he recited vows. "The Penitent," yes. That would be the name of the work.

So she said, in the context of her religious impressions, "Then you must pray that you will not."

Now she had startled him. "I thought you believed in luck," he challenged.

"Ah, well, there may be a connection for all I know," she said merrily. "Come, Simon, cheer up, my dear."

"Yes, ma'am," he said, so aglow in the sunlight that her injunction seemed to have been instantly and miraculously obeyed.

On the way back to the house still (again?) with the bubble in her breast and that sense of a benign mantle embracing her, Mrs. Moffat said to herself in so many words, flat out: *I love that boy.*

Dinner on the porch for three this Thursday was calm and peaceful. Zan had tales to tell, but she told them objectively with only tentative personal conclusions. She said she thought she had a lot to learn about Los Angeles. Simon said little; he smiled whenever he could. There was a truce on.

DEAR SMITTY:

Why don't you start looking around for a car? Probably we can head south early next week. I'll come there on Monday.

I'm staying here only over Sunday. It'll be my last chance to go to a party just as if I . . .

Hands tore off the page and crushed it into his pocket.

DEAR SMITTY:

I'll pick up a car Monday morning and come by for you. I'll have to finish some things I'm doing here for Mrs. Moffat and tell her a decent good-bye.

You locate where the medicine's available. *Do that!*

AL

He folded the page and threaded it through the crack at the bottom of the door.

The next day Zan was off again, meeting business people, all to do with her permanent transfer. It was one of the days that Simon left the place and found his dinner elsewhere.

At the table this night, Mrs. Moffat realized how deep Zan was in plots and plans designed to wring from this city whatever it was she wanted from it. Wasn't there something lacking?

In her bed, Mrs. Moffat remembered Simon's implication that he had already hurt people. It didn't really bother her, because who had not? She did believe that he would need a lot of luck—as would anyone else—not to do it again. And he had responded; he had understood; he had "cheered up"; he had accepted. But where had Zan left any room for luck in her scheme of things? She had alternatives at certain crossroads. If *yes*, then *this*; if *no*, then *that*.

Mrs. Moffat had a dream vision of a programmed computer. *Zan has all the fun too soon,* she thought, feeling cross.

Saturday Zan departed early to go sailing, then take dinner and spend the evening with Nicky Pomerance.

So Simon and Mrs. Moffat, left with the car, were as busy as mice when the cat's away. They did all manner of piled-up errands, and solemnly she chose the hibiscus plants. Simon put them in the ground. Nothing as common as pink and red. Pale yellow and bright bronze, she had chosen.

In the peace of the evening Simon said, "I almost asked you to let me drive this morning, Mrs. Moffat."

"Good," she responded at once. "You are getting used to the traffic then. I know that you are not going to run away from the company tomorrow either."

"No," he said, "I can't do that. Alexandra said we ought not to be rude"—he watched her slyly— "because rudeness doesn't please you. She said she would try to mend *her* manners. So when she wanted me to be her guest—"

"You accepted, of course. The only gracious thing to

do. Yes, I'll be her guest, too. We should all enjoy ourselves." His head was bent. She didn't want him sad.
"Your manners have always pleased me, Simon," she
said.

"It's funny, though." He ran his fingers through the
tight bright curls on his head. "That's twice she mentioned manners. I haven't been thinking about *them* at
all. The last thing—"

"Somebody caught you young and taught you well,"
she said fondly.

He looked up. "Oh, my mother used to *pound* on
manners, just *pound* them into me. But you know ... I
got to be ashamed of them, for a while. *Ma'am?*"

Mrs Moffat had choked, and he was alert to her
distress.

"I must have swallowed ... Excuse—" She began to
cough.

"Shall I bring some water?"

"Please."

He went into the kitchen where he almost never went.
(He almost never came beyond a six-foot margin on the
porch under her roof. He never touched her or her pos-
sessions. He never was that kind of bother.)

She heard his voice and Polly's. He came back with the
glass, and Polly came fussing.

Mrs. Moffat drank. Polly soon departed, satisfied. But
Simon kept watching anxiously.

Well, then, she must say something to blunt or turn
aside his intuition. She wasn't ready for it. "Do you know
what would please me very much?" she croaked feebly.
"If *you* were to drive us to church tomorrow."

Simon sat down. "Yes," he said, as if he were thinking
about something else.

She cleared her throat a time or two. Mrs. Moffat faked
this aftermath of coughing.

"You always go to church, ma'am," he said, in a
moment. "Do you believe that people never really die?
Good people, I mean?"

"I can't explain that," she said gently.

"But do you think, for instance, if somebody killed

himself, that would fix it so there wouldn't be a chance?
I'm thinking of a person who went to church quite a lot
and didn't think that you ought to be afraid."

Mrs. Moffat took hold of her nerves and sighed artful-
ly. "There's no use being afraid," she said, "but these
things are mysterious. Simon, I thought I told you once
that I'm not wise."

"To me," he said gravely, "I don't care what you call
it. What if I want to think about what *you* think?"

"Then you may be foolish," she said affectionately.
"*I'll* never understand a suicide, never. I have to say to
myself, 'Well, God knows'—and let it go at that." She
was trying to be honest, but trying to be helpful, too, and
painfully confused in her mind, obligated by her heart
. . .

"I'll tell you this," she rallied and blurted forth. "To
think on your own death too much—especially when
young—seems very rude to me. What are you saying to
God? 'Okay, You put me here alive on this earth, didn't
You? But You won't catch *me* having any fun out of it.
Oh, no, *I'm* going to gloom around and fret myself into
misery and woe, because You're not telling me all Your
secrets. I won't play unless You do!' " She pursed up her
mouth and held her chin high.

Simon's eyes rounded. Then he burst into laughter,
uncontrollably delighted. Then he said, bent over and
holding his middle, "Oh, Mrs. Moffat, I just love you! I
really do!"

"Now *that* sort of thing is more to my taste," she said,
rocking and nodding. "Ah, well—I'm afraid—I'm getting
to be a regular old sundial, Simon, counting only the
sunny hours."

"I know!" he cried, dashing his mirthful tears from his
eye corners with a bent knuckle.

She could not bear it. She began to act like a very old
lady, which was her privilege, fussing about her sleep, the
fatigues of today, the ideals of tomorrow, dredging up
aches and pains she hadn't used in weeks.

She got away.

Upstairs, the rituals of preparation for sleep seemed too formidable at the moment, and Mrs. Moffat sat down in her flowered boudoir chair to pull herself together.

She and the bearded boy were in some delicate entanglement. He expecting her to heal him somehow? And she too tempted by the fun (oh, yes, the fun of that) to resist trying?

But Sally Warren, her neighbor—a good woman for all Mrs. Moffat knew to the contrary, a sound-enough citizen —was a raw-boned Western farm girl, with a horseface and a raucous voice and a habit of pounding her thigh while bent in a fit of booming—not to say vulgar—laughter. Was she the mother to pound into a small son the sweet old-fashioned courtesies that a gentleman should show a gentlewoman?

It really did not—and the brain knew it—seem probable.

But then, who was he?

It must have been half an hour later, that Saturday night, when Mrs. Moffat went into the bathroom across the hall from Zan's room. She began to close the blind and saw a light in the upper story of the green stucco house next door.

When she had her nerves under control, she went to the phone in her bedroom and called the police. Mrs. Moffat then bethought herself of certain people who need not suffer grievous shock, by night, in the event of noise or gunfire, and she went downstairs, through the lighted hall and the darkened other silences, to Polly's room.

That done, there was still Simon.

"Oh, don't—don't—don't go out, Mrs. Moffat. No, no, no, no—I'll go."

"You are not dressed," said Mrs. Moffat, who was, and made for the back porch.

The moon was on the wane; there was still enough light so that she could proceed without the beam of the kitchen flashlight and be sure that there was no one in the open on her lawns. Anything could be crouching in the borders. It was remarkable, she thought, how being abroad at so unfamiliar a time could change the aspect of so familiar a place. It was exhilarating. She had to use the flash down the shrub-enclosed way to the cottage door. She tapped with her cane and called, "Simon!"

"Ma'am!" His response was quick.

"There's somebody in the Halloran house. I've called the police. I didn't want you wondering."

She heard the springs of the bed, feet thump the floor.

"Wait," he said angrily. "You shouldn't be out in the dark alone."

Then he came, wearing his sneakers and his work pants. He went beside her, walking between her and the far menace, one arm extended horizontally from the elbow, so that there was something Egyptian in her progress.

Polly was on the porch. Simon opened the door, thrust Mrs. Moffat within, told her to lock the screen and stay there in the dark. Then he went, swiftly running and bending from shadow to shadow, toward the north boundary. So the two old ladies, with the house dark behind them, waited on the dark porch, straining to see and hear.

After a while narrow fans of light began to spring up on the property next door. They played like hoses over the shrubbery. They seemed to split and multiply. Very soon Mrs. Moffat's lawns, as well as the grounds of the houses on the next street over, were being washed and probed by light. It seemed that not a leaf could tremble unseen. The display was beautiful, fantastic, beautiful. It seemed that the lights had caught something. There was shouting.

When at last a policeman came toward the house, Mrs. Moffat saw he had Simon in tow.

"Mrs. Moffat, is it? You know this man?"

"Well, of course," she said.

"Staying in the room off your garage, is he?"

"Yes. Certainly."

"He says you woke him."

"Well, of course I did. After I had called you."

"Why was that, Mrs. Moffat?"

"Really, officer," she said. "We are two old women, and he is a strong young man. He went to protect us, officer. Did you see anyone, Simon?"

"I couldn't say, ma'am."

Another policeman came and said, "Somebody's been in the bed out there. Checks out."

"Okay."

"I didn't call you to come and search my guest room," Mrs. Moffat said sternly. "What's happened next door?"

"Somebody got in there all right. Looks like it may have been a vagrant looking for a place to—uh—bed down and maybe something he could hock. Could you tell if anything was taken, Mrs. Moffat?"

"I could not," she said. "I don't know the house well. What will you do now?"

"We'll leave a watch, but he's skedaddled. Very unlikely that he'll come back."

Mrs. Moffat felt the weight of known statistics hanging on the sentence.

After a while there were no more lights, no noise. The men had gone.

"Everything's quiet now, Mrs. Moffat, so will you excuse me?"

"Thank you, Simon," she said.

The man had climbed out of the compost pit and was sitting on the edge of it. He was laughing, as if to himself, not very loud.

"They left somebody watching," said the red-bearded boy. "You can't go."

The man said, "She moved the sundial. So it could be we're going to dig up Gran's pearls just like we figured in the first place. Don't blame yourself, Al. How could you know?"

"You can't dig them up *now*. There's a cop someplace."

"Sitting in a car. So the pearls can wait." The man turned over and, belly to the ground, began a slow crawl.

"I've got an urge to see what my relations look like after all this time."

"Where are you going?"

"Just around. I'll be back."

He vanished.

About 2 A.M., when Nicky brought Zan home at last, the house was silent, its inhabitants abed; no trace remained to be seen of the excitement.

Zan and Nicky kissed and murmured; he walked her up to the stoop. Her key worked. She held the door ajar and watched him go.

Then standing in the wedge of light that escaped from the hall, Zan was suddenly overcome by genuine panic. She was afraid of the night, the trees, the leaves, the sky, the dark, the earth, the air, the smell, some sly and evil rottenness, reminder of decay.

She jumped over the threshold and closed the door, with a wild heart shaking her whole body.

Chapter 10

ON Sunday morning Simon, in his brown suit, shone with cleanliness. Every bit of honest soil had been banished from the crevices of his hands.

Zan had heard what had happened last night. It didn't seem to mean much. When she heard what was going to happen this morning, she said she hoped it was safe to life and limb, but she gamboled out to the apron before the garage looking smart and pretty, in a green-blue costume, showing no signs of anxiety. Mrs. Moffat, in her pink, climbed into the back seat, and Zan got in beside her. Simon was the chauffeur.

The moment the car began to move Mrs. Moffat relaxed. Obviously he could handle a car. She was touched (and a little dismayed, too) to notice that he drove exactly as she did. He turned as she always did to go out the long driveway forward instead of backward. He took the quiet Sunday morning streets at the pace she took them. He parked in the church lot as near as he could to her usual place.

It was her instinct, as they disembarked, to accept his performance as nothing surprising, not even worthy of mention.

Crystal and Claire were waiting on the church steps. There were greetings for Zan and Sunday nods for Simon. It interested Mrs. Moffat to watch Zan take over and by her deportment indicate that she was not in the least perturbed over Simon, but accepted his presence as nothing surprising, not even worth the lifting of an eyebrow.

Crystal and Claire had their favorite spot. The other three were ushered to Mrs. Moffat's favorite pew, halfway down the left side. The old lady went in first, then Zan, and finally Simon, as was proper.

102

The organ was playing. One was supposed to meditate. Or glance at the order of worship that the usher supplied. Mrs. Moffat began to compose herself toward worship. Zan, she knew, although perhaps nobody else could tell, was casting curious glances all around, seeing how the other half lived.

Then suddenly, Zan twisted and touched Mrs. Moffat's arm and then drew herself out of the way as Simon leaned around to whisper, "Please, may I go and wait outside, Mrs. Moffat? Please, may I be excused?" She could see his face, his eyes frantic—a dampness on his brow . . .

"Are you ill?" she whispered. "Shall we all leave?"

"No, no," he said. "No, I don't want that. No, *please.*"

"Why, of course, my dear," she said. "You must do whatever you need to do."

He scrambled out of the pew, past a couple on the aisle side, and went so swiftly away that he might as well have broken into a run.

Mrs. Moffat met Zan's querying eye, shook her own head slightly, settled her shoulders, ignoring the rippling of curiosity all around her, and looked down at the paper in her hand. She noted the anthem for today, noted the text—Matthew 8:2. "And, behold, there came a leper and worshipped him." Her mind began to go on from old habit to imagine what the minister was going to make out of that. (Sometimes she guessed right, and sometimes he fooled her.)

But Zan leaned to whisper in her ear, "Nervous reaction to having driven the car, do you think?"

"I don't know," said Mrs. Moffat.

She didn't. She began to pray.

Crystal and Claire, who had seen him leave the church so precipitously, were consumed with curiosity. When the services ended, they almost battled a way to Zan and her grandmother. It was Zan who turned them off coolly, saying "Oh, he'll be all right," and then she went on to coo, as Zan knew how to do, of course, and before Mrs. Moffat realized what was up she heard Zan promising to bring her by during the afternoon, because Zan would so enjoy a chat and Mrs. Moffat had been saying the other day she hadn't seen them for much too long and she'd love to.

Zan put her young arm under Mrs. Moffat's wing to help her down the six stone steps. Ah, well . . . Once on the level the old lady's eyes were searching, searching. She walked as fast as she could into the parking lot.

His bronze head shone like a torch to guide them to the car. As they approached, he opened the door of the tonneau.

"Do you feel better?" said Mrs. Moffat breathlessly.

"I'm all right, ma'am," he said gravely. "I was just afraid I might embarrass you."

"Shall Zan drive?"

"I'd like to, ma'am, if that's all right?"

Zan got in after Mrs. Moffat, in a thunderous mood. *"Embarrass* you?" she muttered.

"What did you think of the sermon?" said Mrs. Moffat, speaking up. She wouldn't *have* hostile mutterings.

"Oh, I don't know," said Zan. "I've never been able to buy all that about only believe and you don't have to do another thing to be saved."

"That's because you can't *imagine,*" said Mrs. Moffat crossly, "what it might be like if you *did* believe."

"Yes, but miracles, Gran. Only believe and you don't get leprosy."

"They can cure leprosy."

"No. They can arrest it."

"Well, *He* cured it, and if you could explain a miracle, it wouldn't be one," snapped her grandmother. "Why did you commit me to calling on Crystal and Claire, pray tell?"

"Well, they asked, and I *ought* to call on them myself. I certainly thought you'd like to go, too," said Zan, all innocence. "We needn't stay but about thirty minutes," she soothed. "We can say we're having company for supper."

"I can't imagine why you think you ought to call on Crystal and Claire when you really don't want to at all." Mrs. Moffat was cross and upset.

"But I do want to," said Zan plaintively. "I may be a heathen, Gran, but I don't have to act like a stinker and hurt their feelings, do I?"

"I'm sorry, dear," said Mrs. Moffat.

Simon drove the car into the garage exactly in the center, as Mrs. Moffat always did. He opened the door for them, stood in decorum. But Mrs. Moffat saw, on his forehead, the beads of sweat, returned.

"Simon," she said, "let Polly give you a plain cup of soup, please do, and then . . . will you rest this afternoon?"

"Yes, ma'am."

Zan said, "You don't want to spoil my party, Simon."

"No," he said.

When Zan backed the car out at two thirty that afternoon, she saw no sign of Simon Warren. He was not visible anywhere on the grounds in or out of his working clothes. Who could tell if he was or was not inside the cottage? Zan made a small wager with herself. She bet he wouldn't show up at the supper table.

Mrs. Moffat emerged from the house and got into the front seat. Zan backed the car out swiftly all the way, arrogantly sure that *she* could steer backward. She said, while her neck was craned, "I'll bet Simon is going to beg off. What do *you* bet?"

Mrs. Moffat said, "If he doesn't feel perfectly well in the morning, I'll send him to Dr. Sebastian."

Only believe, Zan thought to herself. *She'll believe anything he tells her.* Zan doubted that an unnamed illness had sent Simon out of the church. She couldn't give her uneasiness a name.

She had been going these last few days on the premise that she herself just might become the catalyst here, so she had gone about her business, carefully keeping a friendly insulation between herself and Simon Warren and, unbeknown to Mrs. Moffat, leaving Polly every day a list of numbers where she could be reached. Of course, not yesterday; they had no telephone at sea.

Nothing had happened. Oh, something, perhaps. She had made Polly very nervous.

Zan's object today was to bring her grandmother back into touch with her own friends, the people of her own generation.

It couldn't be good for Mrs. Moffat to have no *other* companion but a young man, twenty-eight years old. Not that Simon seemed that old. What a child he was compared to Nicky. Zan found herself already leaning on Nicky's judgment. Perhaps a man could sense in a man what a woman couldn't. Then she remembered Ben Guest and his venom. Yes, but *he* was jealous. Zan wasn't feeling easy.

Her grandmother said, "Would you mind, Zan, not going into the affair of the police at midnight?"

"All right, if you'd rather not."

"I'd rather not be asked a million questions, none of which I can answer." Mrs. Moffat sighed. She did not seem at ease.

Crystal and Claire lived in an old apartment building where the rooms were spacious but the windows mean and small. Zan privately thought it was a dreadful place, gloomy and airless, all compromise.

Crystal was aflutter in her elephantine way. She was very broad of beam, was Crystal, especially from the rear. Zan, who tried to feel sorry for her, must forget all that and consider the deep furrows across the broad, pale forehead.

Claire was like a baby chick when wet—manifest bone. She seemed no more afloat than Zan had found her before.

Alexandra was looking so *pretty!* Where in the world had Marguerite been, naughty girl! Wasn't it a *shame* that Joe and Flo couldn't join them! Now, they must have tea.

So tea was poured with much mention of heirloom china.

Poor things, thought Zan, remembering her brilliant yesterday, the sea, the salt, the sky, the "fun" people at the marina, and the fine finale at Nicky's.

As soon as it was not too soon to mention him, the subject of Simon came up. Had he felt unwell this morning? Everyone in church had been concerned. Crystal and Claire had been asked many *questions*. But Crystal, who was speaking now, did not really care whether he had been unwell. She went right on to ask what Alexandra thought of him. So extraordinary, his beard. Of course, these days . . .

"He seems to be a nice boy," said Zan, her smile tinged with instruction toward tolerance.

Claire was the only one who didn't notice this. "I've been trying to remember the Warrens, Marguerite," she complained, tilting her head, her bony beak aslant. "I must have met them. Of course, it's been years . . ."

"I remember them very well," said Crystal. "She was a large woman."

Zan thought, *For God's sake, how large?*

"Tall," said her grandmother.

"And he was on the rabbity side, although I merely glimpsed the man. What did he do, Marguerite?"

"Insurance," said Mrs. Moffat.

"Do you know," said Claire, "all I can visualize is their cat?"

"Mercy," said Mrs. Moffat.

Zan perceived that her grandmother, who had not wanted to come and did not want to stay, was hard pressed to behave to the contrary and reduced to one word at a time.

"I remember the cat, of course," said Crystal, as if she had been accused of forgetting. "An enormous black cat, Alexandra. I am not superstitious, but I must say that animal had a baleful eye. I don't like slinky creatures anyhow." Her face shuddered, and she reached for the sugar.

"He was beautiful," said Claire dreamily. "His name was Mr. Calico."

"Oh, no, dear," said Crystal, who seemed under a compulsion to contradict her housemate's statements. "It could not possibly have been calico. He was *not* a calico cat."

"Or a gingham dog," said Mrs. Moffat glumly.

The ladies laughed. (*Oh, poor old women,* thought Zan.)

"The cat's name, as I recall," said Crystal, "was Caliban. Yes. You must remember, Marguerite."

"I don't," said Mrs. Moffat.

"What became of the cat, Marguerite?" asked Claire.

"I haven't the slightest idea," said Mrs. Moffat, rousing. "For all I know, she is alive and well and living in Bryn Mawr, Pennsylvania."

Zan managed to laugh and yet conquer the giggles. (Oh, darling Gran beat all, she did!)

"They are still there?" asked Crystal, looking worried. "Simon is going East to see his family soon, didn't you say?"

"One of these days," said Mrs. Moffat, diving into the teacup.

"Do you know," said Claire, "it couldn't have been Caliban if the cat was a girl. Isn't that a boy's name?"

"Nevertheless," said Crystal, nibbling her lips in an anxiety to have been right. (Claire was *maddening* when she took a notion to be logical. Obviously Crystal considered this *unfair.*) "I believe that Caliban was the cat's name. Marguerite can simply ask the Warren boy, can't she, and settle the question once and for all?" Crystal laughed gaily.

Zan spoke up before this childish controversy could proceed further and inquired for the little bird. Crystal sighed voluminously and began to tell about the demise of Quasimodo, the parakeet, reaching for cake to help her survive the recollection of old sorrow.

Zan, who knew that Mrs. Moffat was just barely able to sit still and survive this visit, took care to ease into the long ceremony of leave-taking that must drag out, lest somebody think you couldn't wait to get out of here.

In the car, Zan said, "They're just the same."

"Yes," said Mrs. Moffat broodingly, "although you

don't know what that is, Zan. I'm sorry I wasn't in the mood for them."

"You're worried about Simon, Gran? You really shouldn't feel so responsible, should you? Have you written to his mother since he's been here?"

"I wouldn't interfere," snapped Mrs. Moffat. "I've lost her address anyway."

Zan said no more. A peculiar suspicion had sprung up in her mind. *Oh, come on,* she chided herself.

Crystal said to Claire, "Marguerite was on absolute needles and pins to get back to her hippie boyfriend. *Tsk! Tsk!* I don't think Alexandra is happy about that situation. She wouldn't let on, of course."

Claire came only halfway out of the clouds. "If Marguerite *is* making a fool of herself, I'm so glad that somebody is there to see it."

Zan drove the car into the garage, stopping it sharply on the mark. "Gran, do you want me to knock on the cottage door and inquire for his health?"

"No, no," said Mrs. Moffat. "Just let him be. Let him be."

Ah so? thought Zan, trailing her grandmother into the house. *She's not so sure his "illness" was a physical illness either.*

In the kitchen Polly said to Zan, "He was just lolling on the grass while you were gone, Miss Zan. I went out to see. But all he said was he didn't see much point to working in the garden. 'Not enough time,' he said."

"Well, well," said Zan. "He may be coming to the party in his store-bought clothes after all."

Simon, in his store-bought clothes, came to Zan's party.

He appeared at the door to the porch politely upon the hour of the invitation. But Nicky had not yet arrived, so the party had to wait to begin.

Mrs. Moffat was rocking easily, beginning to be reassured by Simon's deportment, when Zan, making small talk, said, "By the way, Simon, there was a bit of argument this afternoon about (of all things!) your cat."

"Pardon?"

"Your family cat," pressed Zan. "Mrs. Darrell claims that its name was Calico, and Mrs. Adams is just as sure its name was Caliban, and you're going to have to settle the issue."

Simon's eyes were alert. The pupils wagged in their sockets.

"It must have been Cal *something*," Zan prodded.

"A cat?"

"That unfortunate animal," snorted Mrs. Moffat, giving her chair an angry push, "had to answer to the name of Mrs. Calabash."

Zan was laughing. "Now how could anyone forget that! You couldn't have, Simon?"

"Small *boys* don't always get on with cats," snapped Mrs. Moffat. "The fact is, *that* cat got on with nobody."

"How did the cat get on when it moved East?" said Zan, still mirthful. "Did it mind very much?"

Simon was looking at her. His eyes had grown shiny and mirthful, too. "Oh, Mrs. Calabash got married," he said airly, "and had nine children, one for each life. I can't say whether she *minded*."

It was Mrs. Moffat who laughed aloud this time.

"And were all the kittens pure white, too?" purred Zan.

Mrs. Moffat jolted her rocking chair. It was as if she were shouting, "Watch out, watch out."

Simon looked at her, then away, all animation fading. "I don't know anything about cats," he said evenly. He gazed out at the lawns.

"Treacherous beasts, the lot," said Mrs. Moffat. "Especially females." She was furious with Zan.

Zan had done something with her jaw that caused attractive hollows in her cheeks. She said lightly, "Well, then let's talk about seacoasts. East is east and west is west, I've heard that somewhere, haven't you? I will admit I was much impressed by the ocean you've got out here."

"An ocean is an ocean," said Mrs. Moffat waspishly. "And the fact is, ours is bigger."

"Does that make a lot of difference, from the shore?" argued Zan reproachfully. "Ah, I hear a car. Don't go away," she cried, and went off through the house to let Nicky in at the front.

"In the summertime," Simon said, his eyes half-closed, "we had a place on the shore."

"Did you, Simon?"

"Oh, yes . . . up near Boothbay." A wave of sadness seemed to wash over him. "My mother, my father, my sister, and I—"

"In the summertime?" Mrs. Moffat murmured.

"It's summer there." He turned his face to her, but his eyes were owl eyes. He stared within. "An ocean is an ocean. There'll be surf and seabirds. They don't care."

Mrs. Moffat kept her rocking in smooth control. What dream was this?

"Mrs. Moffat," Simon said, "I have to go away from here."

"Where will you go?" she asked lightly. She had said this once before. When he hung his head and didn't answer, she spoke up in heavy disappointment. "For pity's sake, Simon, don't *you* make me wonder all the rest of my life whatever became of you. That's what Tommy Moffat did."

His head kept hanging. He had his left hand curled into his right palm, the fingers of his right hand were folding and unfolding. "I wish I really was your grandson."

"Well, you're *not*," she said crisply. His head came up. "Although I don't suppose that matters too much," Mrs. Moffat went on in a moment, thinking aloud. "Zan isn't *really* my grandchild. She's my young person, just the same."

Now his head was flung back so that he seemed to be looking down his astrakhan chin at her. He sent his rocker into a tiny complementary rhythm, seeming suddenly content.

No, he was not her grandson. Neither was he Simon Warren.

Simon Warren never had a sister.

Chapter 11

THE moment Nicky Pomerance appeared the party became a success. Mrs. Moffat could not help being pleased
with him. He was a man who seemed easy in himself,
urbane, adjusted, lacking any compulsion to put his own
virtues on anxious display. He paid Mrs. Moffat a proper
deference, which was not a hypocritical sweetness or even
any deep interest in her, but simply friendly and proper.
(This made for easiness.) He was just as casual with
Simon, accepting him without apparent curiosity. Mrs.
Moffat was somewhat tickled to suspect that Nicky kept
the edge of his thumb on Zan.

Zan had provided cocktails; the food was her choice.
She teased Nicky for being an amateur chef; he took
teasing well. If he had been warned off asking the "usual"
questions of Simon, he didn't mind answering them about
himself and told tales about strange things people had
wanted to know and how often the facts had been cast
aside for more powerful fictions. The topless ladies of
ancient Crete, for instance, had never yet been topless in
the movies.

Mrs. Moffat, enjoying all this very much, kept a sly eye
on the others. Zan wore an air of proprietorship. (*This
man is mine.*) It was only a little disturbing to notice that
she was showing off her property not so much to her
grandmother as to Simon Warren. Simon didn't seem to
notice. He listened. Sometimes he put in a remark that
went to show how well he had taken the meaning.

Who is he? Mrs. Moffat wondered. (She'd worn out
shock some time ago.) No rustic, that was obvious. Over
and above his manners, his vocabulary when he let it
out, his ability to understand whatever words were spo-

ken—there was something more. Something fine drawn. And vulnerable?

Although they lingered at the table, supper was long over by the time Nicky mentioned his daughter.

Mrs. Moffat found herself startled. Had she known this? Yes, she had known at least that he was a man who had been divorced. She said, "I didn't realize that you had a daughter, Nicholas. How old is she?"

"She is going on fifteen years old, if you can believe it. I see her very seldom, Mrs. Moffat. She lives in Connecticut with her mother."

"Connecticut?" said Simon in the tones of one who hears a very familiar word.

"The last I heard," said Nicky, "she wants to get married. Such is the ignorance of youth."

Zan said, "Look who's talking. He was a child bridegroom himself, Gran."

"So I conclude by arithmetical processes," said Mrs. Moffat.

Nicky said, "How old was Tommy Moffat?"

"A child of twenty," said his grandmother. "But you must remember that when you are in those perilous years, you really believe that you know everything, and of course, as far as you *know*, you certainly do."

"If you wait quietly," said Zan in a moment, "and let that go around again, it will begin to mean something."

Simon had his head turned toward his right; he seemed to be looking dreamily at Zan's profile.

"But don't let her do anything so stupid, Nicky," Zan went on.

"How do I 'don't let her'? An absentee father, further handicapped by his own record."

"Tell her mine," Zan said. "A ghastly enough warning."

Simon put the eight fingers of his hands flat on the edge of the table. Now he stared straight ahead and sat as still as stone.

"Perhaps you don't realize, Simon," said Zan informatively, "that Tommy left me flat more than seven years ago."

He stared at her with owl eyes.

"Nobody waits forever," Zan said flippantly. "So I've seen to it that in the eyes of the law he is dead, do you see?"

"No." Simon pushed his straight chair away from the table; the legs stuttered on the floor, making ugly sounds.

"You, I take it, have seen him recently?" Zan kept her voice calm.

"No," said Simon, cringing. "I can't. Please, may I leave the table? Excuse me? Excuse me?"

"I asked you once before about him," said Zan sharply, "and you didn't answer. Do you *mind* answering?"

The atmosphere had turned ugly and tense.

Simon raised both trembling hands. "I beg to be excused," he said in a fainting voice. "I can't ... stay. Please, Mrs. Moffat? May I go, Mrs. Moffat?" He gazed with owl eyes at empty air.

"But of course, you needn't stay," said the old lady, "although I'm sorry."

He rose; the chair legs grated harshly on the floor once more. He seemed to try to form another phrase, but then he choked and turned and was gone in an instant.

After a beat or two of silence Zan said angrily, "Gran, will you now admit that there is something very wrong with that boy?"

"He may have had a shock."

"What shock? He knew I was Tommy's wife. Why won't he answer my question?"

Mrs. Moffat said, "He answered."

"He sure didn't, Gran."

"He said No."

"But not to the question," cried Zan. "You must be just a little off your darling old noggin if you think he's behaving normally. Look at today. He ran out of church this morning. Nobody knows why. We're not allowed to ask. Now he runs out on the party, in some kind of emotional twit, which is ridiculous! If everybody got up and ran away from a common everyday shock or surprise ... Either he answers a few questions, or you are going to have to get rid of him, Gran. Isn't she, Nicky?"

Mrs. Moffat pursed her mouth. She said nothing; neither did Nicky, who was lying low.

"I haven't told you this before," said Zan, "but when your Simon speaks to me without you around, he's not quite the same fella. Believe me, he *isn't* the sweet little naïve neighbor's boy that you think he is."

"I think," said Mrs. Moffat, "we must apologize to our guest—"

"Oh, Nicky knows all about it!" said Zan impatiently.

"Indeed?"

Nicky said smoothly, "I wouldn't say I knew all about it, Mrs. Moffat. But I do know that Zan has been worried."

"I see." But Mrs. Moffat felt furious. So Zan had been talking about her grandmother's private affairs behind her grandmother's back. Well, Zan didn't know all about it.

And how *could* the old lady explain to them anyway? They both would call her a crazy old fool if she said she hadn't the slightest idea who he was, but to see him happy was such a great pleasure that she didn't care. Oh, no, they'd never understand that or what she'd seemed to herself to have been doing. However, it meant something to her. And surely, if there was a risk, it was *her* risk.

But here was no risk. Simon had said he was leaving, and he might, but Mrs. Moffat would not be told what *she* must do by ignorant children.

Nicky was asking, "Where are his parents, Mrs. Moffat?"

"Still in Pennsylvania, as far as I know."

"You have the address?"

"I threw it away on an old Christmas card list."

"What is his father's first name?"

Mrs. Moffat closed her eyes, pretending to search her memory. Nicky was in the business of finding things out, she remembered.

"I believe he was called Harry. But perhaps Larry. I did not know Mr. Warren very well, at all."

"Do they know where Simon is?"

"I don't believe they do."

"And why not?" cried Zan.

"Really, Zan," said her grandmother. "Times have changed. He is not an infant."

"But don't you think," said Nicky, "he may be a bit of a mama's boy?"

"Oh?" Mrs. Moffat inclined her attention toward his judgment.

"It appears to me that he's on the childish side. Been to the wars, has he? Is no longer sustained by the group mystique. Taken temporary refuge from the demands of the economic world—with, forgive me—a mother figure."

"That may be very clever of you," said Mrs. Moffat wearily. She thought it was gibberish, probably. Or perhaps if you let it go around again, it might begin to mean something.

"You betcha," said Zan. "So why won't he tell me anything about Tommy Moffat? What has that got to do with his mother *or* the demands of the world—which, by the way, this kid is going to satisfy by piddling around in people's backyards." Zan burned like a candle in a pumpkin.

"It's possible," said Nicky with soothing calm, "that your—uh—Tommy has been walking on the wild side and this boy doesn't want to betray him. He may be afraid that Mrs. Moffat would be upset. She has been very good to him, and no doubt he's grateful."

"What a pretty little idea for a story," said Zan ferociously, "full of the most up-to-date human motivations."

"Well then," said Nicky, "why don't you tell *your* story, with all modern improvements, of course?"

"Then there was this cat," said Zan.

She began to tell Nicky all about the question of the cat's name. Mrs. Moffat didn't listen.

By the time Zan had finished, the old lady had marshaled her arguments.

"May I ask," she said cutting in deliberately, "*why* I must now get rid of him? Because, feeling unable to sit through a church service, he very properly asked to be excused? Or because, after fifteen years, the name of a cat was not on the tip of his tongue? I was in the same case myself. Or is it, because, just now, not knowing what he ought to say, again he asked to be excused? Where, in all this, is the menace, or whatever it is, Zan, that you fear so much?"

Zan was biting her lower lip. Nicky's face was superbland.

Mrs. Moffat gave him a stern look because it seemed to her that he was enjoying himself and ought not to be. "Simon has never done me any harm," Mrs. Moffat said, "or threatened to. He has been unfailingly thoughtful and undemanding, and very pleasant company. He has done useful work. He keeps himself immaculate. He is no bother."

"He's too damn good to be true," said Zan.

"It is impossible for me to send him away. If you can't understand why," said the old lady spunkily, "that doesn't matter to the decision. It *is* impossible, I say, and I will not do it. Certainly not on some unfounded suspicion of yours, Zan."

"What you mean is you'll do as you please," said Zan, "no matter what I suspect."

"Yes," said Mrs. Moffat. "Exactly."

Nicky got up. He said smoothly, "If I may be excused, Mrs. Moffat, I think I will say good night, leave you now, and thank you for the pleasure, and hope you have not been too fatigued."

"Good night, Nicholas. Yes, this is tiring me."

Zan's face was studying to be a gargoyle. "I'll see you off, Nicky," she said.

"You betcha," murmured Nicky.

Left alone, Mrs. Moffat moved to her own rocking chair. She set it into slow motion, thinking stubbornly, *How I got into this entanglement is of no consequence now. I have meant the boy no harm. To cast him out, because I'm afraid of him—that would do him harm, and it isn't even true. I am* not *afraid of him. I will not do what I think I ought not to do. I will not be scolded either.*

She had forgotten to snatch up her stole. The air was fresh and growing chilly. The little creatures were still.

She could not hear the little voices. She waited, as she was. He would know where to find her.

As she waited, a tension and an oppression seemed to lift away with a rustling of leaves.

Out at the front, Zan was blazing. "A fine-feathered friend you turned out to be! What's the matter with you, Nicky? Couldn't you darned well see that the poor old darling is head over heels in love with the creature? She's got some delusion that she's terribly important to him. Oh, I can be understanding, if that's what's wanted. I betcha it *is* pretty exciting when you are seventy-four years old and all of sudden here comes a young male who hangs on your every word and butters you up day in and day out. But what's the end of it, Nicky? Can't you see she's heading for some kind of mess? He can't really be in love with her."

"Tell me," said Nicky coldly, "what's all this about being in love? For which read sex, eh? You're being plumb silly, Zan. Or else jealous."

Zan had become stiff as a stick, in the semidarkness.

"I'd be careful, if I were you," Nicky said. "I'm not sure it's your grandmother's neck that's reaching for the strangler's hands. I'd sooner get between a dog and a bone than between a man and his mother figure."

"Oh, balderdash!" Zan spit out at his theory.

"*I'm* not going to help you force her to kick him out," said Nicky coolly. "You can't do it, and it's stupid to fail. You ought to shut up and behave like a dutiful grandchild and know your place, and that'll get you farther and protect her better, and I don't know what's the matter with *you* that you can't see it."

He gave her shoulder a small slap, got into his car, and drove away.

Zan went back into the house. Her grandmother was out there in the rocking chair. Zan bit hard on the insides of her cheeks, until they hurt, and she was in control of any outward signs of her fury and frustration. She went out, took up the soft woolen stole, placed it gently around the old lady's shoulders. She bent and kissed her grandmother's hairline, where she always had. She said nothing, turned back, crossed through the sitting room, and trudged upstairs.

But she did not turn on the light in her bedroom. She settled at the window.

Gran is a foolish old woman. She has been taken in. She is enchanted; she won't listen; she won't see, doesn't know what it's all about! She likes him because he says "ma'am" all the time! Anybody can say "ma'am."

Well, then. Zan wouldn't go back to New York at all. The hell with it! She would stay right here, right here on guard, until he had been got rid of. She'd stay and she'd force—

Or else she would go back to New York and stay *there,* and the hell with it! And Nicky Pomerance was a rat fink, and he could whistle for Alexandra Terry.

Her eyes began to ache from straining to distinguish the exit from the path to the cottage. How did she know he was in the cottage?

Zan gave up watching and held her skull in her hands.

The brain inside was not sixteen anymore. It was twenty-five years old. It knew what childish emotions were rippling along some surface or other, masquerading as thought. But the cold brain sat in the skull, and coldly it said, *Alexandra, you are making a jackass out of yourself. Why alienate a man like Nicky! You may need him. Why antagonize the old lady? To what end? Is it worth it? . . . .*

Look at you, threshing and writhing! Like poor old fat Crystal, you've got to be right? Is that it? Or are you agonizing because you long for . . . you hunger and thirst after something you won't "believe in" because (although you don't know what it is) you know you cannot have it?

In the dark kitchen of the Halloran house they were fighting. The red-bearded boy was thrown against the gas range; metal rattled. The black-bearded man staggered and slipped on the vinyl floor. They rose; they fell, arms flailing.

Then the man was hunched over the sink, whimpering. The boy was backed against a cupboard, panting.

The man said, "Quit with this. Quit, will you?"

"You started it," said the boy. "You had to crawl on your hands and knees under the gold dust plant and listen in on Alexandra's party. So you found out you're dead. *I* didn't do it."

"Alexandra, Alexandra." The man turned on the water and put his head under the gushing faucet. "God Almighty, my leg is killing me." He straightened, dripping. "Get me a bottle of bourbon out of the bar, will you, Al?"

He limped heavily into the Hallorans' living room and put himself down on a brocaded sofa, wet head and all. The red-bearded boy brought him the bottle.

He said, "Smitty, you never bought the medicine. You spent all the money I gave you. You haven't got any medicine left."

"So what?"

"So your case stops being arrested. Sooner or later you'll get contagious."

"Why don't you tell Alexandra what the gook doctor told you?"

"Stop it. Stop it," said the boy sadly. "I'll see if I can find some of the medicine tomorrow," he said in a moment.

"You do that, you do that. It's a hell of a thing, you know," the man said.

"Listen, Smitty, if you want, I can try to find the pearls before daylight."

"No," said the black-bearded man. "I can go right to them. After all, I put them there."

"We ought to get away, though."

"What's your hurry? When have I had it so good? Only thing missing—"

The boy cringed.

The man drank deep. "You know, I think you're right, Al. I like the whole name, too. Alexandra," he said in the dark.

The red-haired boy went out of the house by the side door. He walked up to a tree and put his face on the rough bark.

Chapter 12

MRS. Moffat came down early on Monday morning, being weary of lying wide-awake in her bed.

Polly said, "Oh, Mrs. Moffat, Simon's got a terrible big bruise swollen up on his cheekbone. He'll maybe have a black eye. I didn't know what to do for it."

"Did he say how it happened?"

"He ran into something in the dark. That's what he said."

"I see," said Mrs. Moffat.

A contamination had come creeping in, a spoiling of her Eden. Polly was anxious, suspicious, confused, no longer in all simplicity pleased to be serving. There was turbulence and there was friction in the house. Zan against Simon. Mrs. Moffat forced to resist pressure. She finished her breakfast, pondering what could be done about this.

Then she took up her cane, went out on the gravel paths, and seeing no sign of Simon's bright head anywhere on the grounds, she made her way to the cottage door and rapped on it smartly.

Simon was dressed in his brown trousers, yellow sports shirt. He let her into his room, which was in order. On the neatly made bed stood his small canvas bag, gaping open. On his face there was, indeed, an ugly bruise.

Mrs. Moffat peered at the injury, took no alarm, but advised the application of ice to reduce the swelling. She then sat down in his only chair, wound her hands together at the head of her cane, and said, "I want you to listen to me, Simon."

He sat on the edge of the bed farthest from her. The bruised cheek toward the eastern wall—and the sunlight pouring through the high square windows on that side of the room, making a nimbus around his head.

"I've been having too much fun," Mrs. Moffat said bluntly. "The time has come for me to tell you just how Tommy Moffat looked to Zan and me. I don't doubt he doesn't look at all the same to you. Oh, that's a great source of confusion, you see. Six of anybody's acquaintances, strung out along the years, might not do much better than the six blind men did with the elephant."

She sighed and launched into a compressed and meticulous version of the events leading up to Tommy's disappearance.

"I don't know whether you can possibly imagine," she went on "how a very young woman, about to bear her lover's child, will feel when he abandons her. The child didn't live, and Zan wasn't sure she herself could go on living either. But she pulled out of that pit."

Simon didn't speak. He had fallen into a deep dreamy mood to receive what was said to him.

"Untrustworthy, unreachable, a man who cannot be held to answer," she said mournfully. "That's not your image of Tommy Moffat, I suppose."

"No," he said. He sighed and threw his head back; his eyes were glittering. "I ran into him in Seoul. I was on leave and—restless. I met up with him and four other guys, his buddies. He was in a restless mood, too. I don't know, Mrs. Moffat, whether you can possibly imagine what a couple of restless guys will get up to, in foreign cities especially."

"I don't know," she said placidly, letting herself fall into a simplicity of listening. "I've read about it."

She pressed the golden knob of her cane into her cheek and remembered earnest male novelists who had made explicit lists of deeds done and sensations encountered. But too many spun off into lyrical gasps, thick with symbols to the point where Mrs. Moffat could make nothing at all of the experiences. Perhaps it was simple. Grab, smash, rip, rape—revenge on all the women in the world (especially one's mother), but Mrs. Moffat had always hoped that negatives alone were not motivation enough. She was willing to concede that she might never really know.

"Smitty was the one with ideas," Simon was saying. "He never ran out. I thought he was great. There was nothing he could dream up that I couldn't do. Oh, Lord—" He smothered the oath or the invocation in his throat.

She said aloud, dryly, "Joe Keating still cherishes his memories of 'Hinky-dinky parlez-vous-ing,' whatever he means by that. I don't necessarily expect you to come to a bad end from such a spree," she went on comfortably.

Simon grinned. Teeth gleamed in the redness of hair. And then he sobered. "Well, this spree didn't come to a very good end."

"How so?"

"Well, after about ten days, I guess it was, some of those people turned on us, and there was fighting, and somebody yelled for cops and MP's. Smitty and I took a big drop—I don't know if we jumped or fell—off a balcony, and his leg buckled. But we went three-legged down the alleys, laughing, you know, like kids and shushing each other, and he said we should get behind this wall and . . . But it was a place we should never have got into."

The boy was not here, but far away. Mrs. Moffat neither spoke nor stirred.

"Pretty soon things quieted down," he said. "Smitty was on the ground in the dark. I said, 'Up. Up. We better get going.' And a couple of the people there came with lights and—and—and I was so . . . God, I was so—I was so shocked and shook, choking on my heart and so *sick* . . . Mrs. Moffat, I ran." He sank facedown onto the bed. "See, I ran and left him. I get nightmares."

"Go on, as soon as you can," said Mrs. Moffat calmly. "Go on. You left him in this place, you say? What happened to him?"

Simon sat up. "I didn't leave him very long." He sounded faintly bitter. "I found the other guys. I tried to make them go with me to get him out of there. But they wouldn't. So I turned him in to the cops—I mean, his location."

"They put him in jail, did they?"

"Not really."

"In the hospital, I suppose?"

"Yes, ma'am."

"You were charmed with him, I take it," she said musingly. "You felt you'd let him down. So if he asked you to come here, you'd feel you must?"

Simon had his hands hooked together by the bent fingers. "You're right. I thought I should come, but," he said, "I should go away now, Mrs. Moffat. I don't want to bring things down on you or on Alexandra. I'll be gone by tomorrow morning. I know what I can do to make it up to you, and I will, I promise."

She felt frightened. "I've known for quite a while," she said, "that you're not Simon Warren. I should have known it the first day."

"P-pardon?"

"You didn't realize the sundial had been moved."

"Where did it used to be, ma'am?" he asked, without guilt, but only curious.

"In the middle of everything, of course," she said impatiently. "But the big tree began to shade it too much of the day. Simon Warren never had a sister. He was a blond. You lied to me."

"I didn't know what else to do," he murmured. "There was nothing else that I could do."

"You had no choice," she mocked, and pulled down her mouth corners. How she despised that phrase—that cop-out phrase—always phony.

The boy was staring at nothing.

She said, with a spark of anger, "Well, what shall I call you? Peter?" (Simon called Peter.)

"That's close," he murmured within his trance. "Smitty calls me Al."

"Smitty is what you call my grandson?"

"Yes, ma'am."

"Why does he call you Al?"

"Lots of people do," He pulled himself into a present decisiveness. "Mrs. Moffat, I don't want you to know my real name. There's a whole lot I don't want you ever to know. It's too bad, and it's too sad, and I just want you to count the sunny hours."

Mrs. Moffat said, "I suppose that serves me right. But what's wrong between you and your mother?"

She thought he wasn't going to answer. Then suddenly and somewhat coldly he said, "She's dead. She killed herself. With pills."

Mrs. Moffat drew in her breath.

"The Navy gave me compassionate leave to go to her funeral. But it was either my fault or my Dad's fault, and I couldn't go to her funeral with him there. How could I go? So that's why I went on the town with Smitty. When you can't stand the way things are, you've got to pretend it doesn't matter. All right. That's chicken."

"You had a choice," said Mrs. Moffat.

"Pardon?"

(*I suppose you think you* knew *that woman, you ignorant child,* she fumed to herself. You *knew what was life and death to her—when ninety-eight percent of her life you'd never even heard of!*)

"You could have chosen to figure you didn't know 'the way things were.' It would have been a better gamble," she said stiffly.

"Everything I do turns out to be wrong," he said, as if he had heard her railing at him. "I've let everybody down. I can't make it up to them. All I want (I told you) is not to do it anymore, and maybe there's only one way, and that's just to quit—like she did."

"Where's your father?" she snapped at him.

"Oh, he . . . doesn't want any part of me. He . . . got rid of me and forgot and got over me. He's married again. He sent me five hundred dollars, but I can't go home."

Mrs. Moffat found herself adrift. Something was wrong with the chronology.

"Simon, how long ago did your mother die?"

"When I was nineteen."

"How old are you now?"

"Twenty-four, ma'am." He put both hands on the top of his head as if they were a cap. "*Don't* ask me any more, Mrs. Moffat. All this time you didn't—you never did—and it was wonderful to me. But it couldn't last. Nothing good can last—nothing."

"Nothing bad can last either," she said briskly. "Go get some ice on your face. And if that doesn't help, you must see the doctor."

Mrs. Moffat rose. Simon got to his feet, head bent slightly to one side as if he listened.

She gave him a haughty look. "That wasn't a question. That was an order."

He let his breath out; he turned for the kitchenette.

Mrs. Moffat was sorting out the sequences. If he had gone on the town with Tommy Moffat at the time of his mother's funeral, then the riot in Seoul had been five years ago. Where had the boy been in the meantime?

She was looking down and could see into his canvas flight bag. It was empty except for an envelope, business size. She read the inscription: Paul Henry Allenstag, Jr. Then the name of a hospital. At the upper left she read Hale Mohalu.

She rocked on her small feet, not yet knowing in full consciousness why.

And somebody was pounding on the door. Zan burst through it. Mrs. Moffat lifted her head high and stared. Simon came out of the kitchenette.

Zan said severely, "You shouldn't be in here, Gran."

Her grandmother said loftily, "Why not, pray?"

"Because," said Zan, her eyes flashing, "he hasn't been feeling well, and he might have something contagious, and if he hasn't considered the risk for you, I have."

Mrs. Moffat looked at Simon, who was holding a tea towel to his face. In the only eye that she could see there was such despair, it was as if she watched the spirit dying.

She said, in icy command, "Zan, go outside and wait. I'll be there in one minute. Do as I say, and do it right away, and close the door."

To Simon she said, "If you think you must go in the morning, then of course you must. And you needn't say another word except one. Tomorrow you must say good-bye and let me wish you luck, which with all my heart I surely must do. Shall I expect you at dinner?"

"No, ma'am," he stammered. "No, I don't think ... I have some errands quite a way from here."

"I see. But you and I will take breakfast together."

She turned her back and marched out of the cottage.

Not bad, she said to herself, paying no attention to Zan, who fell in at her side and seemed to be exhorting or explaining or apologizing.

That, Mrs. Moffat went on to herself, *was a pretty fair recovery and rather decent behavior for an old lady who leads the sheltered life you lead.* She knew now what had so rocked her.

Mrs. Moffat had the habit of forcing herself to pronounce (correctly or not) an unfamiliar place-name, so that she would recognize it again. A word she had not seen on that envelope was sticking in her mind. Kalaupapa, on Molokai.

A peninsula, as she saw it, with surf and seabirds. Three churches, one of them Father Damien's. A tiny jail, a fire engine, cottages rent-free. A few more than two hundred people were still there. Many could have gone back into the world, but they preferred not to try to cope with so much prejudiced loathing. They would stay where they were until, one day, there would be nothing left but cemetery stones.

New patients were treated at Hale Mohalu, in Honolulu, for what was now properly called Hansen's disease. She remembered the subject of the sermon yesterday. And Simon's fierce cleanliness could be fear.

She could not know, of course, whether the boy was a leper. She could see no signs; she might not know all the signs. He could have spent the five missing years at the place of treatment. She thought perhaps Tommy Moffat was there, even now. The house the two of them had stumbled into in Seoul must have been a house of lepers, or why, when "the people there came with a light," had Simon choked on his own heart in such terror?

It was a disease that disfigured. Although surely, surely, it was not so easily caught—what, in a few minutes or even hours? Mrs. Moffat had read that this was an ancient superstition.

A tremor was rippling up and down her back—here in the morning sunshine. Was it not written, unclean? Unclean!

Ancient superstition was not cast out in a few minutes or even hours—no.

Zan had her by the arm and was shaking her. "Gran, you're not even listening. What's the matter?"

They were at the porch door.

"I'm sorry," said Mrs. Moffat.

Not a word of this to Zan. Not a word. The decision made itself; her mind closed on it with a snap. Because Zan must go elsewhere for the night. But Zan would not leave Mrs. Moffat here, if she knew. She would not go elsewhere by herself and be safe. She would stir up authorities, uproar and turbulence. But Mrs. Moffat had other procedures in mind and things to accomplish during this day. Zan must go soon.

"I'm trying to decide," said Mrs. Moffat. "Go eat your breakfast, and then we'll *talk*."

Nicky Pomerance, being busy, had snatched a sandwich in conference. He came back to his own office at one fifteen to find that Zan had been calling him persistently.

He dialed the number. It was the Huntington-Sheraton Hotel.

"Zan, what are you doing *there?*"

"Oh, Nicky, Gran threw me out." He could hear the feather edge of hysteria in her wailing voice. "I had to get out. I'm about frantic. Could you please come over here as soon as you can?"

"Honey, I'm up to my neck—What do you mean, threw you out?"

"She *did*. She said that I must go. She said I didn't understand, and she couldn't explain things she'd known all her life so that I *would*. She said she didn't have time. Simon is leaving tomorrow, and there are certain things she simply has to do, and it's like life or death.

"I didn't know what to make of it! I tried to calm her

down. I tried to get her to take a pill. I wanted to call the doctor. But she was furious, Nicky.

"She said I was intolerably presumptuous. It was her house and not mine. I had no business jumping to the conclusion that she didn't know what she was doing, and no right in her home if she didn't want me there. And that's true."

Zan was crying.

"Look, Zan, I can't get away. Why don't you take a cab here? By the time you arrive, I can manage a coffee break."

"No, no, I can't leave this phone. He's gone somewhere. But Polly's going to call me when he comes back."

"And then what?"

"I don't know. That's why I need—"

"Where did the Warrens go in Pennsylvania?" His businesslike tone steadied her.

"Bryn Mawr."

"How long ago?"

"Something like fifteen years."

"I'm going to do a little checking."

"Oh, yes—do."

"And I'll get to you as soon as I can—say between four thirty and five. *You* take a pill. Take a nap, Zan."

"I'll be okay," she said on a long breath, quietly.

Zan went to the window and looked out at the broad acres, the lawns and terraces, and scarcely saw them.

She knew very well that she herself had forced her grandmother to that final cruel plainspeaking. She had rejected even a trial belief in what the old lady was saying. She had been outraged by the thought that her own protective instinct, based on loving concern, so pure and sound, could be ignorant and destructive.

But now Zan felt lost and miserable, having perceived that her "instinct" was partially based on a conviction of superiority, for which she had no warrant, and it was also otherwise mysterious to herself. She did not understand why she was overreacting. She could not name a specific possibility to fear as much as this. Murder, was it? No, not murder. Maybe it wasn't fear that she felt.

She was obsessed. She could not stop her mind's picturing their two heads. The old lady's with the knot on top, the profile dainty and turned up somewhat saucily. And the boy's strangely beautiful helmet of bright hair and the uncanny sweep of the color around cheeks and chin. The head bent graciously, the face grave, as if he were old and she were young, he were wise and she were frivolous.

No, no. Zan caught herself embroidering symmetrically. The point was not which of them was wise or foolish, old or young. The point was that they were in a state of gentle companionship, ageless, and too innocent to believe. One of the desperate needs of the human heart is to trust somebody, and no questions asked. Zan, who could not, could not bear to see such risk taken, such punishment asked for.

Chapter 13

AFTER Zan's taxi had come and she had departed finally, although not before she had stirred up poor Polly to
vigilance (as Mrs. Moffat knew and deplored), the old
lady took a hasty bite of lunch very early and went up the
stairs.

She paused at the top to listen to Polly snicking the
locks on doors and windows, sighed, for there was no use
forbidding this, went into her bedroom, sat in her favorite
chair, and took up the phone.

Simon had left the property on foot—to do whatever
errands he needed to do. Mrs. Moffat was sure he would
return to say good-bye. She had figured out what to do in
the meantime.

She dialed the area code for Boothbay Harbor, Maine,
then the numbers that would give her information there.
She asked for the phone number of Paul Henry Allenstag. A summer inhabitant. In a twinkling she had it. She
was not surprised. A junior had a senior for a father.
Peter was "close" to Paul. The nickname could also be
Al. In Boothbay it was summer; Mrs. Moffat was pleased
and excited.

Her finger plodded through all the numbers.

"Hello?" a woman answered.

"Mr. Paul Henry Allenstag?"

"I'm sorry, he isn't here. This is Mrs. Allenstag. Can I
help you?"

"My name is Marguerite Moffat. I'm calling from California. Tell me if there is a son, a Paul Henry, Jr.?"

"Why, yes. There is." The woman's voice grew cau-
tious.

"Mrs. Allenstag, I am seventy-four years old. Your step-
son is a friend of my grandson. He has been here at my

house. I'm worried about him. I feel his own people ought to know where he is."

"Oh, that *is* kind of you, Mrs. Moffat. We *have* been worried. He ought to have been home long ago. My husband is at his office in New York, but he's commuting to the house in Westport, although he usually stays in town in the summer, and he hasn't come up for the weekends at all. Perhaps you'd rather talk to Paul's father?"

"No—I think to you. Please bear with me. Mrs. Allenstag. It's important." Mrs. Moffat thought the woman sounded openhearted and ordinarily kind, at least. "Did the boy's mother kill herself?"

"No, no!"

"*No?*" said Mrs. Moffat sharply.

"Well of course, she did take too many sleeping pills, but it was one of those accidents. She was caught in the pill cycle, you see. One to pep up, one to calm down—one for every mood."

"There wasn't a death wish?"

"Oh, who knows, really?"

"Her son thinks he knows. Thinks it's *his* guilt. Or his father's."

"Oh, I'm sure *not*. Paul, he was in the Navy—an honorable place to be—and sons are let go, don't you think?"

"I do agree," said Mrs. Moffat approvingly.

"And his father is not to blame for being what his father is. If she couldn't cope with the life she led, she should have revised it. I don't mean to speak ill—I am not to blame, Mrs. Moffat—especially since I didn't meet my husband while his first wife was alive. Nor is Gretchen to blame. Gretchen's the daughter, a darling girl. She was only twelve at the time. Give me your address and phone number. I'll tell my husband. I'm sure he'll do *something*."

Mrs. Moffat gave the information. She said, unsatisfied, "You think he'll do something? But why does the boy think his father wants no part of him?"

"Oh. Well. Is it possible you haven't heard? I suppose it is. That seems strange. It—let's see— must have been soon after his mother died that young Paul defected to the Communists and made tapes and motion pictures for them, and said terrible things about this country, and hideously embarrassed his father, who's in Wall Street, you see. Of course, the charitable thought is that they brainwashed him. Some people think he oughtn't to have succumbed, but I wonder what *they* know about it."

"But how did he get *out?*"

"The story is they just let him sit in some prison camp for close on five years, and then one day, without warning, they dumped him over the border. I guess he was no more use to them."

"I daresay he was never much," said Mrs. Moffat grimly. "That kind of treason is getting to be obsolete."

"What?"

"You can hear it on TV just about every evening," said Mrs. Moffat. "What an evil place this country is and how all its institutions need destroying. Quite the 'in' thing to advocate subversion. Why wasn't his return in the news?"

"Oh, the military snatched him up and put him in a hospital in Hawaii and debriefed him. I thought they seemed disgusted and determined *not* to let him hit the front pages."

"Who seemed?"

"A Dr. Enoch Grant, the one who phoned us. Paul's father sent five hundred dollars for tickets home. That was almost two months ago. It's been a suspenseful summer. I've—never met the boy."

"I hope," said Mrs. Moffat, "that you get to meet him."

"Oh, but surely—"

"You must tell his father," said Mrs. Moffat, "that he is carrying such a staggering load of self-reproach that he is more than half convinced that the whole world would be better off without him in it."

"Oh, don't," the woman said. "Oh, keep him there until his father gets there. Oh, no—that shouldn't be. It's unfair. It punishes living people too much—too much."

"I agree," Mrs. Moffat said.

She rested a few minutes. Then she put in a call to Dr.

Enoch Grant at the hospital in Pearl Harbor. He was not there. Messages were left: he was to call a certain operator.

Mrs. Moffat took off her dress and stretched out on her bed, but she dared only doze. She must pick up the phone when it rang. So she let chunks of information tumble through her mind like a child's blocks. The temptation was to build with them, put them in sequence, and call it consequence.

Shock of his mother's death, fear of his guilt in the matter, sent him on the town.

Tommy Moffat (with the best ideas) had charmed him into excesses; they had pushed the fun too far. The boy had made two of the three legs of the fugitive pair, mirthfully staggering the alleys. Hiding behind the wall in the dark until the shocking sight of loathsome faces had sent him running in uncontrollable revulsion. Guilty of *this*, he had tried and failed to rescue his friend, and at last, because he could do no better, he had betrayed his friend to the authorities. Bogged down in shame, he had drifted across borders with disreputable people and been snatched up for a prize victim and had weakly succumbed.

Ah. Too simple. Too, too simple. Too much was discarded, unregarded. If his mother had been caught up in the pill cycle, then no specific resolution to take too many was necessary. The whole stupid and futile regime was suicidal enough. But people can dig their own graves with their teeth at the table, and often do, and whose guilt is that?

Tommy Moffat was no consequence of anything that Simon had ever done, no punishment. Tommy Moffat was bad luck, walking.

And as for the brainwashing—the brain by clever pressures altered, "opinion" grafted in—Mrs. Moffat thought that had had a very brief vogue. It could have had a political value commensurate with the trouble taken for a very short period of time, when only a few knew that this sort of thing could be done, but a great many did *not* know and so could be fooled. These days there was a

more generally accepted and universally applied understanding of psychological principles and, in fact, it was
quite difficult to give forth a didactic opinion even in the
parlor without friendly neighborhood analysts concluding
you must "really believe" something else.

Opinion. Opinion.

Come now, she thought sleepily. *Let us formulate
Moffat's law.*

Hm. Everyone walks carrying a hoop of his own hori-
zons, large or small (since scales differ) and more or less
illuminated by his own understanding. What resemblance
or relationship his world has to the real one, none can
know. But the one sure-thing bet is this: The world I
"really believe in" *does not, it cannot, it never will coin-
cide with reality.*

And the great glory of this law—of course! of course!—
was the prevalence of loopholes!

Mrs. Moffat's phone rang.

"Dr. Grant here."

"Oh, yes, Doctor. I am Dr. Moffat." Well, she had a
question. She'd have to lie to get an answer. "I need a
fact or two about Paul Henry Allenstag, Jr. You exam-
ined him, didn't you?"

"Yes, Doctor. Underweight, listless, malnutrition, obviously. What's he doing in California?"

"What's the reference to leprosy?"

"Oh, that!" The doctor, so far away, had a strong
laugh. "Well, I don't blame you for getting the straight of
it. Seems a doctor on the other side, some sadistic type, I
guess, told him that's why they were putting him over the
border. Said he'd contracted it and they didn't want to be
bothered, so let the Americans deal with it."

"That was a lie."

"Sure it was a lie. He was a pretty mixed-up kid.
Didn't know who to believe there for a while."

"I keep getting the impression that leprosy's in the
picture somehow."

"Well, this gook doctor must have had access to what
they wrung out of him in the first place—five years ago.

You must have heard about his buddy, Doctor. His buddy, the leper?"

"The point is this, Doctor," she snapped. "I need to know whether or not in truth his buddy *was* a leper."

"Why, certainly. The minute they picked him up with his leg smashed, they shipped him quick to Hale Mohalu."

Mrs. Moffat said nothing. Her lips were dry.

"How's the Allenstag kid doing?" Dr. Grant inquired, in a voice that was subtly less cordial and open.

"Not well."

"That's not surprising," said Dr. Grant. "If you ask me, he dug himself a hole and pulled it in after him. He'll never get out."

"In your opinion, he doesn't deserve to?" she said. "Well, thank you, Doctor."

"Women!" she heard him say, and then, "Where are you calling from Doctor? I would like to follow up—"

She hung up and slithered down toward the foot of her bed, pulling the afghan high around her shoulders.

She was old and cold, and her bones ached. She had gone to work and found out what the boy hadn't wanted her to know, and it was bad and sad. If Tommy Moffat was being so horribly punished, *she* didn't know that he deserved it. Poor child. Poor child. As for the lad who was Simon to her, she could not even imagine whoever would get him out of the pit that he was in. Unless, under a name that was a lie, and safely out of traffic, he had been able to stay here every day and play in the garden. She wanted to cry, but snuffled valiantly instead.

Ah, well, either his father would come here before his son went away, or his father would not. And if his father did come in time, he would know what to do, or he would not.

And Zan was safe, after all. And there was another chunk of information.

At the time of that riot in Seoul, at the time of the house of the lepers—and before—*before* Simon had so much as laid eyes on Tommy Moffat, that man was *already* a leper and cared nothing—oh, nothing cared he—for danger to the health of *his* buddy.

This was too sad, too bad to think about.

She moved her head on the pillow restlessly and slipped over into another world. She was so fond of that boy. They had such delightful times. She remembered the day they had watched a colony of ants for an hour and a half. Mrs. Moffat in a garden chair, absurdly using her opera glasses, and Simon on his belly, and the two of them giving the mysterious little creatures names like Busy Boy and Isobel and the pallbearers—she remembered them—as plain and as clear as could be.

She had *not*, she remembered, with the tip of her cane "created" a "Chinese wall" around their city, thus becoming their luck.

She must remember Moffat's law. She had, in fact, two points of view. There was the strict array of links and chains, cause and effect, reward and punishment, where all her deeds and choices had accumulated until she stood on good repute as on a coral reef, and how gratifying that could be.

But there was another way to squint up her mind. A mode she had lately known quite often, when one may adopt a heady willingness to take whatever is given and call it neither reward nor punishment and so snatch up delight and any lucky thing, knowing that, just as if it were love—were love—you don't have to deserve it.

The afternoon was getting on. Zan said on the phone, "Well, you see, Mrs. Adams, unfortunately I have this engagement to spend the night with a friend, and I also know that she feels just a little ashamed not to have called you and Mrs. Darrell for so long, and she probably won't. But my grandmother is going to be feeling in need of company this evening. *I* wondered if you might drop in casually, all the same. And not say I asked you? She'd be so pleased. Well, you see, Simon Warren is leaving tomorrow, and she *is* going to miss him, I'm afraid. I had thought of calling the Keatings. Do you think I should?"

The red-bearded boy trudged along the sidewalk. His bright head caught the eye of a passing motorist, who glanced back over his shoulder to look again and saw no one on the sidewalk.

The boy was threading through the stand of shrubs along the Hallorans' driveway. He darted across to the side door at ground level. It opened to his touch.

Nobody was in the house. He looked everywhere. He put his package of medicine on the coffee table in the living room. He sat down in a wing chair in a corner to wait.

Mrs. Moffat slept until almost six o'clock, which was a scandal.

She washed and dressed in her blue and went down, apologizing. Polly said she'd tiptoed up to see two times. Dinner was on the stove. It could be held back. Everything was under control. And Simon had not come home yet.

Mrs. Moffat said that she did not expect him for dinner. She would dine in half an hour, please.

She sat down in her rocker to wait, nevertheless.

The man had no scruples about breaking out the screen on one of the windows at the back of the cottage with the spade. He dropped the tool over the high sill and came head first and tumbled awkwardly to the floor. No one was in the place.

He crossed to the window on the other side; he could just see through a maze of branches his grandmother's back porch. He thought there was movement. A rocking chair?

Oh, well, broad daylight. He had a pint in his pocket.

He sprawled on old Mr. McGregor's bed to wait.

Nicky paid the waiter from room service and brought Zan her drink.

"Now," he said, "take it from the top."

Zan was very much subdued and showed no sign of hysteria.

She described the morning's events, beginning with the cottage. "I don't know what he told her. He must have told her something. He told her he was leaving. I'm sure of that."

"All to the good, not so?"

"So it would seem."

"Why so depressed?"

"It depressed me to look at myself," she admitted. "Such a befuddlement and a confusion of values."

"Go on."

"If I'd believed that Gran is in physical danger while that boy is there, then nothing, absolutely nothing—no names she could call me, no insults—could have made me leave her. And if I didn't believe that, I ought to have gone quietly when I was asked."

"Sounds like a reasonable analysis." Nicky drank to that.

"Reason has nothing to do with this," Zan said. "I'm afraid. It's emotion. I don't know what I'm afraid of. My heart sinks down with a sickening slide—I don't know why.

"I've got my finger on the house—an ear in the house. I spoke to Polly. He is not there now. Not expected for dinner. Crystal and Claire and Joe and Flo all will be dropping in there this evening. She should be safe until they leave. But that's only a reasonable assumption. Not necessarily true."

Nicky was staring at her. "You fixed it so the old lady isn't going to get a last quiet evening with her young friend, eh? Seems to me you must believe something."

Zan put down her glass and held her skull with all her fingers. "About nine thirty I want you to drive me there."

"And then?"

"I'm going to sit outside at the back, watching, until the sun comes up."

"What good is that?"

"I don't know, but I'm afraid."

"For God's sake, Zan, call the police."

"What would I say?"

Nicky drained his glass. "Never did I expect to hear

such illogical girl talk coming out of you," he said. "But
—it has its appeal. What can I do but come sit, too?"

"All right." Zan's smile was radiant. "And that's darn
sporting of you, Nicky."

"Well," he said, "could be there's a little something I
haven't told you, that has revised my thinking to a degree. The boy who's staying with your grandmother is not
Simon Warren."

"No?"

"I spoke to the real Simon Warren myself, on the
phone to Bryn Mawr."

Zan seemed to go into a trance. "I'll bet that's what he
told her. I'll bet that's what he told her this morning. She
wouldn't care, you know."

"Why wouldn't she care?"

"No, no. No, no. I understand that. She just doesn't
care."

"You *understand* that?"

"Yes, I do!" Zan said, blind-eyed.

Joe and Flo and Crystal and Claire descended on Mrs.
Moffat before the dark came down. Polly was delighted to
see them.

The day had been so warm, hadn't it? Marguerite's
porch was wonderfully cool. Where was her guest, the
Warren boy? Was it true that he was leaving?

Mrs. Moffat replied that the day had been somewhat
warm, but her porch was wonderfully cool. The Warren
boy was out. Yes, of course, he was leaving, and how had
they guessed? Had someone told them?

"Oh, Marguerite, you will miss him, won't you? Such a
nice boy—you say."

In a way, Mrs. Moffat admitted, she would miss him;
yet in a way she would not really.

Polly turned on the lamp that hung over the table and
the lamp that stood behind the settee.

The black-bearded man crept out the cottage door in
the new dark and crouched low to see past the stems of

the shrubs. The porch was lit and full of people. He squinted and stared intently; not one of them was Zan.

The red-bearded boy slept in the wing chair and now and then whimpered.

Zan searched the hotel room for extra blankets. The night might turn chilly. Nicky had no overcoat; Zan no woolen garments. Their mutual resolve to do something as silly as what they were about to do had cheered them enormously. They were full of quips and laughter.

Joe and Flo and Crystal and Claire left at nine. Mrs. Moffat come back to the porch, where Polly was collecting glasses, and gazed out toward the dark cottage.

"You'll be sitting up, I suppose," said Polly.

"No," said her mistress. "I didn't sleep at all last night, and I must be up early in the morning. So I'm going to bed now. You must be tired, Polly. Don't wash any dishes. Go to bed, do."

Mrs. Moffat locked the screen door. She went into the sitting room and locked the double-glass doors. The sitting-room lights went out. Polly put the porch light out and went into the kitchen and locked the kitchen doors. The kitchen light went out.

In the Halloran kitchen the red-bearded boy dashed cold water on his eyes.

Chapter 14

THE phone rang in Zan's room.

"Miss Zan! Miss Zan!"

"Yes, Polly. Yes? What is it?"

"He's in the yard. He's digging! He's digging like he's digging a grave. I didn't see him come in, but there he is—digging. What shall I do?"

"I'm coming, right away. Don't let him in the house. Don't let him near Gran. I'll be there in two shakes."

Polly let her instrument clatter into its cradle. She was in the front hall. She looked fearfully up the stairs. She turned suddenly and tottered on her old feet, and crossed the small square space to the door of Mr. Moffat's den.

Upstairs, Mrs. Moffat had removed only her dress and put on her dark-blue tailored robe, since there was still the possibility of Simon's father appearing—how far into the night she could not guess. She tied the dark-blue sash firmly. She had heard every word that Polly had said.

She plucked her flashlight from the bed-table drawer and marched down the stairs. To her consternation Polly, in a sack of a nightgown and nothing else, was standing in the door to her husband's private place, holding his gun in her shaky old hand.

"Put that down," commanded Mrs. Moffat in ringing anger. "What is the matter with you? It's only Simon out there. He's not digging any grave. I know exactly what he's digging for. Sit down before you fall down, and try to behave yourself."

Mrs. Moffat marched into the sitting room, using the flashlight instead of stopping to light the lamps.

She unlocked the double doors, crossed the porch,

unlocked the screen, and stepped out into the freshness of the night. She had her shoes on; no need to shuffle in bedroom skippers, but she had forgotten her cane. Ah, well, it was not really dark. Best, she thought, to go by the bounce of the city lights on the high dome of the sky than to use her flashlight close ahead of her feet and blacken all the rest of the scene.

She could see him, a colorless figure in this light, bent over the spade, bearded chin to his breast, moving in jerky rhythm. Stabbing the ground with the blade of the spade, stepping back, and making shallow scooping undercuts to strip away the sod, there in the very center of the back lawns.

Oh, yes, she knew what he was after.

But it was very sad.

Tommy Moffat had been a child, aged eleven, the year that he (and Simon Warren?) had stolen his grandmother's jewel box, and he had thought as a child. How pitiful that he still did think as a child and had sent this "Simon," within a boy's adventure story, to find what he had thought was treasure, her beads and things.

The original pedestal of the sundial had been deep-rooted, so they had left a column of concrete in the ground. She could hear the spade clink-clank against it. The digger crouched to grope with his fingers in the loosened soil.

Mrs. Moffat's eyes were full of tears because this was so sad.

"Oh, no, oh, no, my dear," she called out, tremulously. "They are not worth anything. I was never a rich enough woman for real pearls."

He sprang up. He was grasping the spade at the middle of its handle with his right hand. With his left he swung at the old lady.

Mrs. Moffat staggered, and lacking her cane, she fell.

Zan, pelting through the house, burst out on the porch just in time to see this happen and then the jumping-jack figure with the weapon in his hand brandish it and turn his bearded face to the sky.

Zan burst through the screen door and ran on the grass, screaming.

Nicky, who had delayed to take the old gun away from Polly, was not far behind. He wasn't at all sure the gun was fit to be fired. It was loaded, but Nicky could easily imagine it blowing to bits in his hand. He could hear Zan.

There was something strangely pure in Zan's screaming. Body, heart, mind, and soul cried, "*No!* You won't hurt her! *No!* You *won't!*"

Blood run cold, thought Nicky, his own feet pounding the turf.

The man was defeated. Bent over, his arms up, curved hands protecting his head, he scuttled, like a big spider, for the deeper darkness.

"Halt or I'll shoot," shouted Nicky, but impurely. (He didn't mean it. The threat was ridiculous!) The man vanished.

Zan was on two knees and one elbow, with the other arm under the old lady's shoulders.

"Oh, Gran, did he hurt you? Does anything hurt you? Are you all right? Oh, darling Gran, please be all right."

"I do believe I'm more or less all right," said Mrs. Moffat slowly. She flexed her right ankle. She thought, *I'll be black-and-blue tomorrow.*

The ground was very hard. Blades of grass prickled the skin at the sides of her neck, which was odd and unpleasant. But her limbs did seem disposed in an ordinary way—nothing awry. "I'm probably catching my death of a cold," she continued dreamily.

Zan began to laugh and cry.

Mrs. Moffat saw him standing high behind Nicky's bent back and over Zan's knotted-up body.

"Simon," she said calmly, "will you please pick me up and carry me? Nicholas has that gun to hold, and Zan's not strong enough. I wasn't rich enough for pearls."

Zan rolled over and bounded to her feet, hissing like an angry tortoise.

Nicky said, "Hold it, fella. Hold it."

But Simon paid no attention to either of them. He

squatted and began to slip his arms gently under Mrs. Moffat, hunching his shoulders against Zan's frantic fists hammering his back.

"Oh, Zan," said Mrs. Moffat. "Let him alone. You don't always see what you think you see."

Nicky said, "Let him alone, Zan." He pulled her away. He held the gun on Simon. This seemed the only solution. He couldn't carry the old lady and hold the gun, too. He dared not give the gun to Zan.

Simon lifted Mrs. Moffat gently and began to carry her carefully across her own backyard.

So strange was this night—so strange.

Zan ran ahead and opened the screen door. "Indoors," she cried.

So Simon put Mrs. Moffat down gently in her recliner there in the sitting room as Zan snapped on lights.

Zan said, "I *saw* it, you know. What do you *mean,* I didn't see what I thought I saw?" She was blazing at Simon.

"Mrs. Moffat," said Simon, "if you're okay, may I be excused?"

"No!" howled Zan.

"Hold it," said Nicky.

Simon glanced at him, curiously.

"All right, he's *not* Simon Warren," cried Zan. "I suppose you know that?"

"Yes, yes," said the old lady wearily.

"Who *is* he?"

Mrs. Moffat rubbed her forehead, moving her head to do so. She was shivering.

"I'm going to call the doctor," cried Zan. "And somebody to come and make some sense. You watch him, Nicky." Zan dashed out to the porch, fetched Mrs. Moffat's stole and spread it over her. Then she hurried the length of the sitting room and was appalled to find Polly still in the hall, bolt upright in the chair by the telephone, looking quite mad. Zan managed to break the poor woman's terrified tension, but she thought Polly must stay very still until the doctor saw her. She found Dr. Sebastian's number on the list and dialed it and stood dancing with impatience until she realized that the phone was dead.

The three persons in the sitting room were silent and motionless.

Nicky had been sensing that the boy wished desperately to speak to the old lady, but dared not, in Nicky's presence. The old lady had suffered some kind of shock, of course. She was struggling with worry. The boy was anxious to get away; before that, he needed something from her. Some reassurance?

Nicky gave it up. Had he been the blushing kind, he would have been crimson from top to toe. He was mortified—disgraced in his own sight. He fervently hoped that Zan had not heard and no one would report around this town or anywhere else the idiotic grade-B piece of dialogue that had come out of his, Nicky Pomerance's, mouth. "Halt or I'll shoot." His spirit burrowed deep, away from the memory. It hid for shame. What a ridiculous command to be shouting in somebody's suburban backyard, while holding a gun that he would not fire on a bet. He had since bethought himself of a very corny epitaph Nicky did not care to acquire.

He didn't know it was loaded. Surreptitiously he had since removed the one and only bullet. Now he knew that it was *not* loaded.

It looked well, however. Zan believed in it.

Simon—or whoever he was—hadn't taken the slightest interest in the gun. Neither had Mrs. Moffat. They had other things on their minds, he guessed. Other things? Who in Hollywood would have believed that? It must be that either they didn't believe the gun was dangerous, or they didn't believe that Nicky was, and they were right on both counts.

Zan came in from the hall, stepping high, like a prancing pony. She said, low-voiced, "Nicky, the phone's cut off. I'll run to a neighbor's. Polly's in a bad way. We've got to have the doctor and the law. So hold everything—okay?"

"Okay," he croaked.

Zan withdrew, dancing backward, saying no more, smiling faintly, behaving as if the silence in the sitting room were precious as fine old china and must not be broken.

They all heard the front door close behind her with a soft thud and a clicking.

"No," cried Simon, electrified. He rolled his eyes toward Mrs. Moffat.

"Then do something," said Mrs. Moffat instantly. "Go help Alexandra."

"Wait. Wait!" But Simon had rushed away, and Nicky was only bleating after.

"Mrs. Moffat," said Nicky, between outrage and pathos, *"tell* me what's happening!"

Her grandmother said, "Zan shouldn't have gone out."

"She went to phone. The phone's cut off."

"Yes. Well, he would know." The old lady shaded her eyes with her trembling hand. Her lips went on moving.

Nicky, still holding the gun, began to run. He passed through the front hall where Polly was slumped in a chair, and let himself out the front door. He jogged down the private walk and saw them to his left on the public sidewalk, racing in and out of shadow; he pounded after.

He reasoned backward. Or upside down or inside out.

There was a man out there.

He was dangerous to Zan.

The phone company had not had trouble on Mrs. Moffat's line so coincidentally.

Who knew where the phone wires came into the house?

Polly had used the phone to say Simon was digging; when Nicky and Zan had arrived ten minutes later, he was still digging.

He had not since been out from under their eyes.

Yes, he had. He had spidered off into the dark.

He never *had* been Simon.

There was *another* man out there.

Zan was up on the stoop of a lighted house. She had her finger on the doorbell button. Simon stood at her back.

"May I use your phone, please?" Zan said to the woman who opened the door an inch only. "It's an emergency. Just me," she added, her head high. The woman let her in and they both slammed the door in Simon's face.

Nicky rushed up behind Simon. "Who is the other man?"

Simon put his arm on the house wall and his face in the bend of the elbow. "I should have known she wasn't rich enough. She wasn't rich enough for pearls."

Mrs. Moffat was not sure where Polly was or how. She would have liked to know. But if Polly felt able, Polly would be beside her right now. Mrs. Moffat did not want to stir Polly to an attempt to do what she was not able.

The old lady was no longer concerned for Zan running to the neighbor's house in the dark. Zan was protected. She was thinking about Zan's shock, to find out where and how Tommy Moffat was. She knew very well that Simon didn't want Zan to find out: Simon had had some romantic dream of coaxing Tommy Moffat far away from here. But could he, without the treasure they'd expected?

Had Simon, under any circumstances, the force to make Tommy Moffat do what all authority, society, science and art had never—

She heard the small whine of the metal spring at the top of the screen door. The floor boards of the porch were old.

She was alone; the shock of her fall still ran in her nerves and weakened her limbs. She was old and afraid.

But Mrs. Moffat shook herself, came smiling up from these waters. Seven years ago she had said certain words to her only grandson. For seven years they had stood, for better or for worse, indelibly her last words. Now there came from the soft dark of an ordinary Monday night the gift and surprise of another chance. Ah, but she would take no thought for what she would say.

"Come in, Tommy," she sang out.

He came.

He was dressed in gray trousers and a gray shirt. The garments were not clean. His shoes were scuffed; the laces were knotted, where once they had been broken. His face was half covered with a black beard; Mrs. Moffat saw, with sadness, a thread or two of gray in it. The beard was clipped close in imitation of Simon's, although it was not curly. Tommy's hair was long and straight; it lay wild on his head, and on his forehead—his forehead . . .

"Where did they all go?" he said.

"To telephone," she answered. "Too bad about the pearls. I think there is almost a hundred dollars in the right hand secret drawer of my slant-top desk. You know where that is."

He limped across the room; it was a bad limp. She was sorry. He opened the desk, yanked out the silly little "secret" drawer, shook the paper money forth, snatched it up, and turned back to her, leaving the slant-top open, the drawer out, his whole deed revealed as having been done.

Now he came close and put his hands on the arms of her chair. His sunken eye was jeering. "Best you can do, Gran?"

Mrs. Moffat put up her hands and touched the deformity of his forehead, not likely the result of disease, but sufficiently repulsive.

She said earnestly, "Tommy, did they help you at the treatment place? Was it in any way pleasant there?"

His good eye flickered, but the little eye, diminished in its deep place, burned steadily with malice. He snatched her hands down.

"So Al told you about the treatment place?"

"No."

"He told Zan?"

"Nobody told Zan."

"I'm an arrested case, you know. I'm not dangerous."

"Good," she said. She didn't believe him.

"Maybe I'll stay and tell her myself. I'm not dead, for instance. I ought to be able to prove that."

Mrs. Moffat put up her left hand to shade her eyes. "Don't stay, Tommy."

"Why not? You don't think Zan would be glad to see me?"

"She can take it," said Mrs. Moffat, "but if she sees you—"

He snatched at her hand and wrenched it away and she

offered him the candor of her eyes. "Do as you like," she said. "You may be right. It's best the hauntings stop. She ought to see her pretty lover's dead and gone."

"Lover," he snarled. He began to wrench at the diamond rings on her third finger.

Her knuckles had thickened; force would never get her rings past that obstacle. The pain was excruciating. Mrs. Moffat hissed with it. "You'll never get them off," she gasped. "If you don't let *me*."

He threw her hand into her lap. The finger was bloody. With her good right hand she wiggled and turned her solitaire, her wedding band of smaller stones, twisting and working them along, as she had to do.

She dropped them into his hand. "These are all the jewels that I own," she said, and wished she hadn't. He wouldn't believe her.

"I'll bet," he growled. He put the rings into his trouser pocket. "I'll make a deal. Send money. Mail it to me in Mexico. Then Zan won't have to know about my trouble."

"That's not going to work," said Mrs. Moffat calmly. "Zan's going to know all about it this very night."

"You're going to tell her?"

"Nobody's going to tell her."

"She thought I was Al out there. He won't let me down."

Mrs. Moffat said, "You can't make a deal, Tommy. but I will *give* you money—not much, I suppose, but something, regularly. For free. For nothing—as long as I live."

He muttered under his breath, words of disgust and disbelief. He leaned very close; his breath was bad, his teeth were brown, and one was broken.

"If they find you dead in that chair, then all you've got I'll get, you realize?"

Mrs. Moffat made her skull heavy on the chair's headrest. She knew he would inherit only the end of his own life; he was almost there, as it was.

"No," she said wearily, "but try it and see. No one could ever tell you anything. Poor Tommy."

Zan's voice rang out in the house. "The doctor's coming, Polly. How are you now?"

Tommy Moffat's neck craned slowly around and he looked over his shoulder. But it was Simon who came into the sitting room.

"The police are coming," he said quietly, and came walking steadily into the room.

"You pushed her, by accident. I wasn't here. Okay?" Tommy said in a low voice.

Simon said, "No." He was braced to leap, to attack, to hurl himself. "Get away from her."

Tommy said, whining, "Break my leg. Run out on me. Turn me in to the cops. Tell me you're going to stick with me. Sure you are. You lousy traitor. Worm your way in with my grandmother!"

He lurched, moving awkwardly but without much sound, through the double doors. The porch floor creaked. Simon kept walking steadily in a straight line to the double doors. Mrs. Moffat heard Tommy make a profane suggestion—what Simon could do to Tommy's wife.

Zan called, "You're not going anywhere, Simon!" She appeared, sprightly as an elf, in the door from the hall.

Simon stopped at the double-door sill. Mrs. Moffat listened, breathless, for the screen door, but a siren screamed outside somewhere.

"The cops are coming," cried Zan with satisfaction, "and we'll get the straight of this. Are you a twin?" she said to Simon, as she went dancing toward her grandmother. "Have you a little shadow, goes in and out? Gran, there's a taxi—"

At this moment Nicky Pomerance came into the sitting room with a burly middle-aged man in a gray suit.

"This is Mr. Allenstag," he began, but the man began to stumble the long way of the room, one hand outstretched.

"Oh, you poor damn fool kid—am I glad to see you!"

Simon was pulled up, his back arched like a Spanish dancer's, his head high, his eyes glittering. The big man's arm went around the boy's shoulders, his cheek to the boy's cheek, the impetus of his rush and his affection carried them both over the doorsill into the quiet dimness of the porch. Simon went with a sudden breaking of his back.

Zan glanced at Nicky, who shrugged and vanished to answer the doorbell. She glanced at her grandmother. The old lady's eyes were closed. Her right hand was cupped over her left hand, and both were held to her breast.

Chapter 15

THE doctor and a policeman had come. Zan had to help old Polly to her bed, while Dr. Sebastian took a look at Mrs. Moffat. He passed Zan when she returned to the sitting room.

"Your grandmother will do," and off he went to tend to Polly.

Zan drew nearer to the others, noticing the white tape covering the third finger of Mrs. Moffat's left hand. She sat down to listen. It seemed to Zan that the policeman was asking questions in one language and Mrs. Moffat and Simon, too, were answering in another.

"So you said you were this Simon Warren?"

"Yes, sir."

"That wasn't true?"

"No, sir."

"Did you know that, Mrs. Moffat?"

"I soon knew it, yes."

"But you didn't mention it to him?"

"No."

"Why not?"

"It didn't matter very much."

"Why did he come here under a false name?"

"He was after my pearl beads."

"Beads?"

"Yes. They were not real pearls."

"Where are these beads?"

"Buried in the yard."

Simon had not sat down; he was standing against the

154

one closed leaf of the double doors, his head in profile to the room. Listening. Mrs. Moffat was listening, too.

Zan had spotted the old desk in the corner. She could feel her nerves tightening and her temper rising. She said, "Her grandson and my husband stole them, years ago. My husband buried them because he couldn't, I suppose, fence them at his age. He sent this friend of his, I think, to dig up the loot."

"Thank you, Mrs.—er—?"

"Moffat," said Zan.

"The chap you call Smitty is named Moffat?" said Mr. Allenstag to his son.

Simon didn't answer.

Zan said, "My husband deserted me more than seven years ago and ran away from the law, but I believe that he's out there now. When he pushed my grandmother down, I took him for this man in the poor light. He has a beard also. But he cut the phone wire. He came inside while we were elsewhere, phoning. He took money from that desk, do you see? And look at her finger! He tore her rings away. My husband is without any particular mercy. I'm sorry to have to say so, but it is true."

"He is a leper, isn't he, Paul?" said Mr. Allenstag.

"Not if he takes the medicine," said Simon quietly. "I bought some today. It's in the house next door. I don't know whether he'll find it."

There was a very deep hush, and then a faint shout outside. Simon slid suddenly around the leaf of the doors and was on the porch. The policeman was after him. The screen door banged behind them. More shouts went up.

Nicky Pomerance went as far as the doors. "Your garage is on fire."

Zan popped up beside him. "The Halloran house is burning! See there?"

"This house?"

White-faced, Zan ran across the porch and backward on the lawn, looking up at the roof, and Nicky followed.

When the doctor came from Polly's room, via the kitchen, Mrs. Moffat was out of her chair, and he, with understanding, gave her his own arm for a crutch. So she attained her rocking chair and, with the doctor's fingers on her pulse, she watched the light.

The strange and beautiful terror of burning structures after dark. Sirens. A fire truck roaring. The police shouting. A crackle of gunfire. An ominous silence.

Zan, standing with Nicky near the sundial, cried out and strained forward. Nicky held her back. A spotlight steadied on the man who had fallen just within the hedge, on Mrs. Moffat's side.

A policeman hunkered down; a man with a red beard came out of the darkness and knelt on the grass. Zan ran to kneel there, too, and Nicky let her go.

"Marguerite, lean back," said the doctor gently. "I imagine I'll be wanted."

"No hurry," she said grimly.

"I don't understand," burst Simon's father, his nose to the screen. "Why should my son be so devoted to this—to this . . . Excuse me."

"Once upon a time, they had a few nights and days during which it seemed to your son that they were joyous and free. There is power in that."

"I'm sorry," he said. "I'd like to thank you. I don't know what to say to you. I'm sorry."

When Zan came in, it was a standoff who would comfort whom.

Nicky took Mr. Allenstag's elbow. They went inside.

Zan darted to the footstool and dragged it across the floor. She sat at her grandmother's feet, holding her head in her ten fingers. In a moment Mrs. Moffat put her left hand flat on the girl's back, fingers opened, spread, palm pressed close. At first the fabric of the dress was cool from the night air, but soon there was only warmth between flesh and flesh, and Mrs. Moffat could feel the living rhythms, the strong bones, the pulsing and being. While

Zan drew from the small, warm, firm hand that held so calmly and so undemandingly and so reassuringly and so lovingly and attentively still, something too wonderful to mention ever.

The fire light died away. Mrs. Moffat's garage and car had not burned. The cottage was half gone. The Halloran house had not been seriously damaged. The knots of neighbors and sight-seers had been dispersed. Not too many plants were beaten down. Fat canvas fire hoses were embroidering the ground. Mrs. Moffat was watching in silence, her hands folded in her lap now. Zan, still beside her, huddled warm against her knees. Sunrise would tell the damages.

The doctor had gone. Tommy Moffat's body was gone. Polly was abed, sedated. Mrs. Moffat was turning black and blue, and certain joints were stiffening, but this was no night for sleeping.

Mr. Allenstag was still in the sitting room, talking with Nicky Pomerance in their civilized voices.

Simon came to the door with his flight bag in his hand. Freakishly it was only scorched.

"Come in, come in," said Mrs. Moffat.

He had her garnet pin in his hand. "Your beads are all over the place," he told her, "and ground into the ground, some of them. But I found this."

"Thank you." The pin was broken and dull with dirt. But time had not touched the day she had opened the jeweler's box and found it new.

"Now you must say good-bye," she said quietly.

"Yes, ma'am, I must say good-bye."

She held out her hand, and he took it briefly. It was just a handclasp. "I wish you good luck," she said, "and good times."

"I'll look for them," he promised smoothly. "Good-bye, Mrs. Moffat."

Zan, gazing up, said, "I'm sorry you are leaving, Paul. I never got to know you."

He said, "I'm sorry it had to happen the way it did, Alexandra," touched her hand lightly and went into the house where his father was.

Paul Henry Allenstag, Jr., was the son of a wealthy man, with stocks and bonds of his own. He could have brought the pearls back, even if they had been real, and paid back the insurance company, too. It might have taken a touch of Quixote. He had the background of the right prep schools and the right clothes, and sports— sailing and skiing—good manners, of course, for old ladies—but a sense of changing styles for contemporaries.

He would turn out to be a certain kind of modern. His energies, held down by five years of paralyzed misery, were on an upswing now, what with better food and a little fun, now and then, and peepings and cracklings of hope—yes.

But Zan was not for him. There are unwritten rules in these matters. At twenty-five, she was years too old for him, at twenty-four. She was too much her own woman, besides. There were many very pretty young girls with the proper training.

Mrs. Moffat, her head to one side, considered this pretty structure that passed for thought. It was not true.

While Nicky, inside, was polite to the boy, the father came out to speak to Mrs. Moffat, saying he feared his son had not properly thanked her, since he didn't yet seem to realize that Mrs. Moffat had told his father where to find him, nor did Paul know she had heard about the so-called treason. "Although that's what you might call ambiguous," the father said, struggling to tone down his personal rejoicing, since he was a decent man. "The doctors who debriefed him were pretty hard on the unforgivable sin, but his seventeen-year-old sister is the mascot for his fan club. *I* don't know what he'll do!" He flashed her an impish look of wild surmise.

Then father and son were gone.

Nicky joined the ladies on the porch. He raised Zan

from where she was huddled and tucked her under his arm on the settee.

"Tommy went for that bullet," she said very softly, into the flesh under his ear. "I could tell. He went for that bullet from the day he was born."

"Could be," said Nicky, rumbling the words into her hair.

There would have to be some rites of finality, tomorrow or the next day. Zan knew. She also knew what she could not have. She had told the red-bearded boy that she was sorry. What harm? He had been sorry, too. But the ghost of Tommy Moffat would stand between them and live forever.

It wasn't that she "couldn't have" such a thing as a sudden, sweet, and mindless need to be near some one man. She feared it. She didn't *really* want it. She wanted it, but only with other things. She wanted Nicky.

Mrs. Moffat, having been released to rock, was rocking timidly. Muffled to the tip of her nose in her gray stole, she felt mousy.

Tommy Moffat had never behaved as she had wished he would. All so bad and sad, and yet Tommy had danced like a demon in the light of the fires—and God knew . . .

Her Simon was lost from the garden now. Linked into his own life between past and future, consequences to overcome, rewards yet to win, ladders to climb. Ah, well, he was young. And, of course, some would say that the boy was found.

But Mrs. Moffat was not young. She knew about Moffat's law. Anyone's puny little conception of the whole *must* rattle around within the vast and awesome reality. Wonders *must* press on all sides, and piercings of wonders be sliding like silver light on unknown dimensions, through and through, at the very edge of the range of the eye, and this was true, and she was frightened and too old to speak of such things because they'd only call the doctor . . .

Alexandra Terry Moffat stirred and said in her clear

young voice, "It's chilly. I don't like the burny smell. Let's go into the kitchen. Polly can call us if she needs us. And Nicky can put the kettle on."

She whisked off to the kitchen to put the light up.

"We may as well do as she says," said Nicky.

"I think so, too," said Mrs. Moffat joyfully.